MAGIC & MALICE

STARRY HOLLOW WITCHES, BOOK 7

ANNABEL CHASE

RED PALM PRESS LLC

CHAPTER ONE

"I CAN'T POSSIBLY GO to school today." Marley flopped onto the sofa with a dramatic flair usually reserved for Broadway actresses and passive-aggressive mothers. Never one to miss out on body heat, Prescott Peabody III, or PP3 as our ancient Yorkshire terrier was affectionately called, took the opportunity to curl up at her feet.

"What's wrong?" I hustled over to inspect her, fearing the worst. Marley never wanted to miss school.

"My stomach and my head," she said, touching each body part she named.

I pressed my lips to her forehead. "You don't feel warm."

"Not a fever," she said. "A headache. And stomach pain."

"Hmm." Marley and I were so rarely ill that I didn't have a lot of experience with treating maladies. I'd need to find the magical equivalents of Tylenol and Pepto-Bismol. I wasn't even sure if I could mix the two, that's how limited my nursing skills were. "Are you hungry?"

She considered the question. "I could eat." She sat up and swung her legs to the side of the sofa.

I studied her closely. "Where do you think you're going?"

Marley blinked at me. "To make breakfast."

"If you're too sick to go to school, then you're too sick to make breakfast."

She frowned. "Well, I'm not going to let you do it. I'm not interested in feeling any worse."

"Hey!" I objected. "I don't mess up breakfast." Not when it involved a box of cereal, milk, and a bowl. Anything else was up for debate.

Marley fell back onto the sofa. "Fine. I'll take the risk. Maybe use a spell."

"I don't need a spell for something as simple as this." I walked into the kitchen and surreptitiously pulled my wand from my back pocket. Okay, maybe a spell was the way to go.

Raoul, my raccoon familiar, poked his head in the window above the sink. His fur was sticking up in all directions and he looked like he'd come straight from the nearest dumpster. *Who does magic at this ungodly hour?*

"Who drops in unexpectedly at this ungodly hour?" I shot back.

He dropped to the countertop and then to the floor. *I couldn't sleep.*

"And?"

And I knew you'd be getting the kid out the door and we could chat over coffee before the crazed clown gets here. It's her day, isn't it?

I laughed. "Yes, Hazel and her Big Book of Scribbles will be here soon." Hazel did her level best to teach me how to read and draw runes. Suffice it to say, she'd have an easier time teaching Raoul, despite his lack of opposable thumbs.

Raoul did a sweep of the kitchen and harrumphed. *Nothing's ready.*

"Why do you think I have my wand out?" I said. "Marley's hungry and not feeling well. I need to be quick."

2

I vote for pancakes, Raoul said. *With burstberries and heavy on the syrup*. He held up a paw. *And a whipped cream face on top*.

I peered at him. "You seem to have me confused with someone who takes orders."

Raoul stared at me with puppy dog eyes—or as close to puppy dog eyes as a raccoon could get. *Pretty please with a whipped cream smiley face on top? I never ask for favors.*

I barked a short laugh. "Raoul, that's all you do is ask for favors. Just one chicken bone and I'll never ask for another thing again. Just this last piece of cake for a poor, starving raccoon." I mimicked his pleading tone.

The raccoon clasped his paws together. *Please? I'd be doing you a favor, really. You need all the practice you can get before Marley's birthday sleepover.*

I froze. "What do you mean?"

She's having friends sleep over for her birthday, right? What do you think they'll expect to eat in the morning? You won't get away with cereal. They'll vilify you.

My eyes widened. "But there will be, like, six girls here."

Then you'd better start practicing, Raoul said. *The party's practically tomorrow.*

"It's not practically tomorrow," I said. "Your sense of time is really questionable."

He shrugged. *I'm a raccoon. What do you expect?*

A few hurried spells later, Raoul and Marley sat at the table, happily devouring stacks of pancakes.

"This was a good idea, Raoul," Marley said. She swallowed her last forkful and washed it down with a glass of chocolate milk. I still wasn't sure what voodoo my child with stomach pain managed to use on me to extract a glass of chocolate milk, but there it was.

I'm full of 'em, Raoul said.

"Raoul says he's full of it," I said aloud. I ignored the

raccoon's obscene gesture so as not to draw Marley's attention to it.

"I hope my familiar is as clever as Raoul," Marley said. She dragged herself back to the sofa, where PP3 continued to rest.

"Marley, let's not worry about familiars until we're sure about your magic," I warned. I hated to be the voice of doom, but we wouldn't know whether Marley had inherited my witchy genes until her eleventh birthday. Because her father had been wholly human, she had a fifty-fifty chance, assuming biology worked the same in the paranormal world —which it probably didn't.

A knock on the door signaled Hazel's arrival. Thanks to Marley's calming presence on the sofa, PP3 barely lifted his head in response to the sound.

I aimed my wand at the door and said, "*Aperio*." The door flew open and Hazel stood on the doorstep with her bag and her red curls bouncing like springs.

"Your laziness knows no bounds," Hazel said.

"That's called practice," I said. "I thought you'd be proud of me."

While I sat at the table, Raoul took the opportunity to return to the kitchen for a sniff around. Apparently, pancakes and chocolate milk weren't enough to satisfy him.

As Hazel retrieved the Big Book of Scribbles from the bag, she noticed the lifeless figure on the sofa. "What's happened to this one?" she asked.

"Head, stomach, probably her spleen, too," I said.

Hazel opened the book to the page were we'd left off during our last lesson. "Let's try to finish this page today," she said. "We've spent enough time on this section, I think. I'd like to actually make progress for a change."

Marley moaned softly from her place on the sofa and I glanced at Hazel. "I don't think I'll be able to focus while my precious offspring is suffering in the background. Maybe we should reschedule."

The mere suggestion that we reschedule was enough to send Hazel into detective mode. She waltzed over to scrutinize the child on the sofa. "Are you sure she's sick?" she asked, looking at me. "I sense a Code Wool."

"What's a Code Wool?" I asked.

C'mon, genius, Raoul interjected. *You're smarter than that. Pulling the wool over someone's eyes. Clowny McCircus over here found a way to make it sound cooler.*

I don't know that it sounds cooler, I said. Nothing Hazel said was of the 'cooler' variety.

Raoul shrugged and climbed onto the neighboring chair. *What do we have here? These look like my scratch marks.*

"No running commentary right now, Raoul," I said. "I'm already trying to manage a lesson and a sick child at the same time."

"Except she isn't unwell," Hazel insisted.

"Am too," Marley said from her prostrate position on the sofa. "Completely and totally unwell." A cough erupted from her.

"Since when is a cough an element of this sickness?" I asked.

Marley coughed again. "It's the weirdest thing. It just started now."

Hazel offered a triumphant look. Sweet baby Elvis. That crazed clown was obsessed with being right about everything. She marched over to the sofa to observe Marley more closely, ignoring PP3's growls of protest. My daughter offered the red-haired witch her most pathetic look in return.

"Let's see your tongue," Hazel demanded.

Marley dutifully shoved out her tongue and Hazel leaned forward to inspect it.

"What is it, Hazel?" I began to feel anxious. Was there a magical tongue disease? What if something was seriously wrong with my child?

Hazel straightened and placed her hands on her round hips. "Your daughter has an acute case of performance anxiety."

Marley and I exchanged confused glances. "But Marley isn't expected to perform," I said. Not to mention that she was an excellent student. She never worried about the quality of her presentations or papers.

Hazel faced me. "I'm not talking about academics. Her eleventh birthday is on the horizon and she's concerned that she won't come into her magic. It's making her feel sick." She inclined her head toward Marley. "Or she's so anxious that she's willing to pretend to be sick to avoid her life until the day arrives."

What do you know? Raoul said. *Bozo is good for something aside from juggling balls and drawing stick figures.*

"Marley, is this true?" I asked. I perched on the arm of the sofa by her head.

Marley forced a cough for good measure. "Everything hurts."

Hazel patted her leg. "You have to remember, Marley, that your mother was a late bloomer. Even if you don't come into your magic on the day, that doesn't necessarily mean you're out of luck. Try not to worry so much."

"My mother was only a late bloomer because her father suppressed her magic in order to hide her from Aunt Hyacinth," Marley replied.

Hazel flicked a dismissive finger. "Details, details."

"And look how that turned out?" I said. "We live in a cottage on Aunt Hyacinth's estate and we're both thriving. Who would've thunk it, right?"

"Rose Cottage is rightfully yours, Mom," Marley said. "Aunt Hyacinth isn't doing us a favor by letting us live here."

I sighed. "Still, we should be grateful. If it weren't for my cousins coming to our rescue and whisking us off to Starry Hollow, I don't know where we'd be now." Most likely dead —a fact I preferred not to dwell on.

Marley's blue eyes brimmed with tears. "What if I never come into my magic? What if I'm a regular human in a paranormal town? I'll be reviled."

"You could never be reviled." I bent over and kissed her forehead. "You'll be so unique that everyone will want to be friends with you."

"And you'll still be a Rose," Hazel said. "Don't underestimate the value in that name, especially in this town."

Marley rolled onto her side and closed her eyes. "If you don't mind, I'm going to take a nap now. Feigning illness has taken a toll on me."

"I would suggest taking your nap upstairs," Hazel said. "Your mother tends to get a bit aggressive during our lesson. She's likely to disturb you."

I scowled at Hazel. "I do *not* get aggressive."

Hazel folded her arms. "I believe that, during our last lesson, you threatened 'to go Jersey on my magical clown butt.' I've come to recognize that 'going Jersey' doesn't mean putting on an athletic top."

Raoul snickered. *Man, I love when you go Jersey. It's my favorite thing next to finding a half-eaten pepperoni pizza in the street and no witnesses around.*

I arched an eyebrow. "That's highly specific."

Marley sat up and scooped PP3 into her arms. "So you're not going to make me go to school?"

"No, I'm not." I raised a finger. "But only today. You're not getting time off from school until your birthday rolls around."

Marley headed for the stairs. "Thanks, Mom. You're the best mom in the history of moms, paranormal *and* human."

Hazel rolled her eyes. "Don't let it go to your head."

Raoul snorted. *Too late.*

I held open the front door to the *Vox Populi* offices, using magic to levitate three latte cups in front of me. Bentley Smith, my colleague and resident pain-in-my-rear, managed to snatch one out of the air before I even had a chance to make it over to the desks.

"How do you know one is for you?" I asked.

Bentley inhaled deeply. "Because I smell the fresh aroma of Daytime Nightmare coffee blended with a shot of Make Him Tolerable and I can only assume you intended that for me."

I flashed a smile. "You know me so well."

Our office manager, Tanya, fluttered over to snag the other cup. "You shouldn't be bringing lattes to me. It's my job to bring them to you."

"You know I love to swing by the Caffeinated Cauldron," I said. "It's part of my ritual."

"Her rituals are any excuse to avoid actual work," Bentley said. The elf returned to his desk beside mine and resumed tapping away on the keyboard.

A loud voice drew my attention to the back of the room, where Alec Hale's private office was located. The editor-in-chief never raised his voice—as a fearsome yet dapper vampire, he never had to—but I couldn't imagine who would dare yell at *him*. My eyes popped when his girlfriend, Holly, emerged from the office and slammed the door behind her. She stormed through our section of the office before pausing to notice the last latte, still floating in the air in front of me. She plucked the cup from the air and sniffed the lid.

"Is that Bittersweet with a shot of Give Me Strength?" she asked.

"Your noses are all ridiculously impressive," I said.

"Thanks." Holly sipped from the cup before disappearing out the door.

Although that latte had been meant for me, I didn't stop Holly from taking it. Whatever was happening with her, she seemed to need the drink more than I did.

The three of us stared blankly for a moment, contemplating the scene. "Well, that was interesting," Tanya finally said. "Should I check on…?" She didn't get to finish. Alec stepped out of his office as though his girlfriend had *not* just screamed at him within earshot of his employees.

"Miss Rose, so glad you could join us," the vampire said in his usual smooth tone. As always, he looked like a million bucks in his custom suit and not a blond hair out of place. Great balls of masculine perfection. Couldn't he have visible earwax or something equally gross? Even his fangs were a turn-on.

"I had a lesson with Hazel and Marley's home sick," I began.

Alec's brow lifted with concern. "Marley's unwell?" Whatever the vampire's flaws—and they were too numerous to list —I had no doubt that he cared for my daughter.

"She's fine, really, which is why I came to work." I sat behind my desk and turned on my computer.

"You left her alone?" Alec queried. "Isn't that an issue for her anxiety?"

"Relax, Alec," I said. "Mrs. Babcock is with her. Like I said, she's faking an illness, so it seemed unnecessary to miss a day at the office."

"Why is she faking?" Bentley asked. "I mean, I would have done that as a kid, but Marley loves school."

"She's stressed about her birthday," I said.

"Oh," they all said in unison. Everyone seemed aware of Marley's impending magic.

"She's a descendant of the One True Witch," Tanya said. "I'm sure the magic will be flowing through her veins soon enough."

"Thanks, Tanya." I tried to focus on my screen, but I felt the razor sharp gaze of the vampire still pinned on me. Finally, I dared to look at him and my heart hammered in my chest. It was still difficult to be in close proximity to Alec, even though I'd made the choice to pursue a relationship with Sheriff Nash. Unfortunately for me, feelings didn't dissipate overnight just because it would make my life easier.

"Miss Rose, I have an assignment for you," Alec said.

I tried to mask my disappointment. Of course, that was the reason he was fixated on me. Work. Alec buried himself in it. If he wasn't busy with *Vox Populi*, he was buried in one of his fantasy novels that Marley loved to read.

"That's why I'm here," I said cheerfully.

"What about me?" Bentley asked. "I'm here more often."

"And why is that, Bentley?" Alec said. "A real journalist would be out finding stories, not in here sipping decadent coffees. Even Miss Rose is ready to go at a moment's notice. No coffee in sight."

The pointed tips of the elf's ears reddened. "I was polishing a story for this week's edition."

"Excellent." Alec turned to me. "Now, Miss Rose…."

I looked eagerly at the vampire. "Yes, sir?"

"I'd like you to cover Hattie Rollins-Mahoney's two hundredth birthday party tomorrow at four o'clock. She'll be expecting you."

Bentley smothered a laugh, while I stared slack-jawed at the editor-in-chief. "You want me to go to what now?"

"A party," Tanya said. "How delightful."

I tried to recover gracefully. "You want me to cover a

birthday party for *Vox Populi*?" I asked. "Should I throw in notes on Marley's upcoming sleepover party for good measure?"

"Oh, you're throwing her a sleepover party?" Bentley asked. "Make sure you stock up on burstberries for the pancakes. Kids expect it."

"No, you should make Wish pancakes," Tanya said. "I have a wonderful recipe I could share."

"Thanks, Tanya," I said. The fairy cornered the market on baked goods in our office.

"The party will be featured in next week's society section," Alec said. "Your aunt insists on maintaining that section."

Of course she did. Aunt Hyacinth loved nothing more than a good pecking order. One of the main perks of being descended from the One True Witch was the family's elite status among other paranormals.

"Who's this Hattie and why is she special?" I asked.

"Hattie is a morgen who has outlived her husband and a couple of her children," Alec said. "She lives on the family's estate at the north end of town. Her immediate family will be in attendance."

"I guess I need to take photos?" I asked. Photographs were not my strong suit. Then again, nothing was my strong suit. I just bumbled along and hoped I didn't screw it up too badly.

"A photo of Hattie would be preferable," Alec said. "Perhaps if you bothered to look, you'd know that half the society pages are photographs."

My cheeks flamed. "Maybe I'm too liberal for the society pages. The hierarchy makes me uncomfortable."

"Says the witch by the name of Rose," Bentley muttered.

I whipped out my wand and poked him in the cheek with the tip of it. "Watch it, Smith. I have a special spell with your name on it."

"When you two are finished with your sibling spat, I shall give you the address, Miss Rose." Alec smoothed his lapel. "Then I shall head out for the remainder of the day."

"Hot date?" The words were out of my mouth before I could censor myself.

"Not unless you mean a hot-tempered date," Alec said. "As I believe you may have overheard, Holly is displeased with me at present."

I was surprised that he was willing to admit that much. "I'm sure it'll blow over."

"Indeed." He managed a smile. "In the meantime, I shall seek refuge in my work."

Big. Shock.

"I've started on my next book and would prefer complete silence," he continued. He grabbed a notepad and pen from my desk and scribbled an address. "Four o'clock. Do be punctual. Hattie may be two hundred, but she doesn't suffer fools gladly."

"Why me?" I asked. "Why not Bentley?"

Alec's mouth twitched. "Wait and see, Miss Rose. All will become clear." He strode out of the office without a backward glance.

"All will become clear," I mimicked, once he was out of earshot. "Yes, as clear as blood."

CHAPTER TWO

AT FOUR O'CLOCK on the dot the next day, I arrived at Rollins Manor, the estate of Hattie Rollins-Mahoney. It was an impressive, asymmetrical Tudor-style house with a steeply pitched gable roof and an elaborate chimney. Streamers flew from a pole atop the chimney, making it look like a turret. It was hard to read from this distance, but I was fairly certain 'Happy 200th' was emblazoned across the colorful material. There were several cars parked in a neat row and I wondered whether I was the last one to arrive.

The moment I rang the bell, a butler materialized. He was bald and stout, much like Aunt Hyacinth's butler, Simon. "Good afternoon, Miss Rose."

"Beautiful day for a party," I said. "You know my name?"

"Of course, miss. You're an expected guest."

"Right. And what's your name?"

"Sampson, miss. Right this way, please." The butler accompanied me through the impressive foyer with its gigantic chandelier, and down a hallway to an enormous portico at the back of the house where the Rollins-Mahoney clan was nibbling on hors d'oeuvres and sipping cocktails.

"Which one is Hattie?" I asked, scanning the group.

Sampson frowned. "The lady in the black kaftan, miss." The butler cocked his head. "Are you quite sure you're a journalist?"

I took his point. There was clearly only one two-hundred-year old woman out here. Hattie Rollins-Mahoney held court in a raised swivel chair that allowed her to over-look the entire party. Her black kaftan was covered in white and red bird silhouettes. She wore her dyed black hair pulled back in a French twist and her dark red lipstick only served to accentuate her weathered complexion. Hattie was clinging to her youth with every product available to her. Apparently, no one in the family dared to tell her that she was making matters worse.

"I can take it from here, Sampson," I said. "Thanks." I approached the birthday girl's chair and cupped my hands around my mouth. "Hello, Mrs. Rollins-Mahoney. I'm Ember from *Vox Populi*."

Hattie offered me a withering glance from her position on high. "Nothing wrong with my hearing. I see you've come empty handed."

My cheeks grew flushed. "It was my understanding that I'm covering your party for the weekly paper."

The elderly morgen leaned forward. "Tell me your name again, dear."

"Ember Rose, from *Vox Populi*."

"Rose, did you say?"

"That's right, ma'am." I swallowed hard. Hattie was almost as tough as dealing with Aunt Hyacinth.

"I would've expected better from a Rose," she said.

I whipped around and surveyed the other guests, desperate to get away. "Why don't you introduce me to your family so that I can make a note of everyone's names for the article?"

Hattie sniffed. "I don't make introductions, my dear. Introductions are made to me."

"I can help you," a woman said, hurrying over. "Hi, I'm Hattie's granddaughter, Lacey."

"Nice to meet you, Lacey." She had her grandmother's dark hair, although Lacey's color still appeared natural. "I'm Ember Rose."

"It's so sweet that the paper wants to cover Grandmother's birthday festivities," Lacey said. "Though I guess two hundred is a milestone to be celebrated when you're not a vampire."

"My aunt is old-school and insists that the society section covers the 'right' families," I said. I resisted the urge to roll my eyes in case Lacey was in agreement with that sentiment.

To my relief, Lacey rolled *her* eyes. "Don't let her demeanor fool you. Grandmother was over the blood moon when she heard you'd be covering the party. Can I offer you a drink? We have bucksberry fizz for the cocktail hour."

"Why not?"

Lacey beckoned one of the servants forward and plucked two flutes from the tray. She handed one to me. "This is from Grandmother's personal stash. Not as sacred as the fizzlewick mead, of course, but then, no one's allowed to partake in that except her."

"Sacred mead?" I repeated.

Lacey lowered her voice. "You'll see. She'll toast with it at dinner later. No one else. It's been passed down from generation to generation and she doesn't believe in sharing it until she's passed on."

I glanced over at Hattie. With her special, private cocktail and social expectations, now she reminded me even more of Aunt Hyacinth.

"You must be the reporter." A young, attractive man swooped between us. "I'm Fitzgerald, Hattie's grandson." He kissed my hand. "I didn't realize they made reporters in your image. I assumed they all looked like Bentley Smith or I would've allowed myself to be interviewed ages ago."

"You know Bentley?" I asked. If I could get dirt on Bentley while covering this party, it would all be worth it.

"He and I dated the same nymph a while back," Fitzgerald said. "Of course, Bentley didn't realize she was seeing us both at the same time. Poor fella was gutted."

Poor Bentley, indeed. He was definitely a one-woman kind of elf. Good thing he'd found Meadow. They seemed really happy together.

"Are you still dating her?" I asked.

Fitzgerald chuckled. "Certainly not. I don't even remember her name. I only remember his because he works for the paper."

Lacey heaved a sigh. "My younger brother thinks it's hilarious to bring home a different girlfriend every week to toy with Grandmother's fragile emotions. He's the only male in the family, so she's desperate for him to marry a morgen and produce an heir."

That also sounded familiar. "You must know my cousin, Florian. Sounds like you travel in the same social circles."

Fitzgerald's brow shot up. "Florian Rose-Muldoon is your cousin?"

"That's right. I'm Ember Rose."

He whistled. "That wizard is a legend. I can only hope to rise to his rank when it comes to…" He paused. "To wooing women."

Wooing was a nice word for it. Wholly inaccurate, but nice.

"I suppose you live in a man cave here as well," I joked.

Fitzgerald's smile faded. "Why is that funny?"

Oh. "It's…not funny. It seems to be what all the wealthy eligible bachelors do."

"If it weren't for Grandmother's overindulgence, Fitz might actually be a decent guy," Lacey said.

"Don't be bitter simply because your own husband wasn't a decent guy," Fitzgerald said.

Lacey's expression soured. "Don't mention Weston, please. Not during the party. If Grandmother hears you, she'll lose her appetite and the whole day will be ruined."

"I'll convince her to eat," Fitz said smugly. "I'm her favorite, after all."

"What's this about favorites?" Another young woman came over. She was a petite version of Lacey with the same dark hair and attractive features.

"Avonne, have you met Ember Rose, the reporter?" Lacey asked.

"I haven't had the pleasure." Avonne extended a dainty hand. "Avonne Beauregard. My husband, Stone, is over on the lawn." I glanced across the yard to where a muscular tree nymph was engrossed in a phone call. He was impossible to miss thanks to his brightly colored top that seemed out of character with the rest of the family.

"It's always work with that one," Fitz said. "Does he never stop?"

"That's how he earns his living," Avonne said. "Not everyone comes from money, Fitz. He's managed to earn it all by himself."

"And a good deal of it at that," Fitz said.

Avonne's smile forced her eyes into a squint. "Aster and I serve on the board of the VWFF together."

"Oh, right," I said. "I've heard her mention that organization." The Vampires Without Fangs Foundation. I decided to quote my cousin and pretend to be knowledgeable and civic-minded. "Vampires missing their fangs is not simply a vampire problem. It's a problem for everyone."

"So true, Ember," Avonne said, appearing pleased. "I

always thought I was the most organized paranormal in town until I met Aster. She puts me to shame."

"She's been working under the watchful eye of her mother," I said. "It's hard not to become an uptight perfectionist under that kind of constant scrutiny." I faltered. "I mean, organized and efficient."

Fitz chuckled and clinked my glass with his. "Welcome to the family, Miss Rose. You'll fit right in."

"Fitz, do you ever stop flirting?" A woman with fair hair joined our trio.

"Ella, this is Ember Rose," Fitz said. "Ella is our cousin."

"I'm Hattie's great-niece," Ella said. "The blond sheep of the family."

"You can thank Ella for helping Sampson to organize the party," Fitz said. "She lives in a cottage on the outskirts of the estate, so she's always over here."

"Not always," Ella objected. "Besides, you live on the property. I didn't see you helping with the party planning."

"I'd have helped with the fizzlewick mead if Grandmother would ever let anyone near it," Fitz grumbled.

A servant came by our little group. "A top up, Miss Lacey?"

"Only if it's a calorie burning potion," Lacey replied. She patted her belly. "Not that anything I use seems to be effective."

I glanced at her seemingly flat stomach. "Why do you think you need to lose weight? You look great."

Lacey shrugged. "A side effect of Weston and his philandering, I'm sure. I have it in my head that there are all these flaws I should fix. If only I were ten pounds lighter, Weston wouldn't have strayed." She shook her head. "Ridiculous, I know."

"If I gain too much weight, I don't need a Weston. My familiar will be sure to mention it." Raoul would have a field day with muffin top jokes or snide comments about objects in the mirror being as large as they appear.

"That's wonderful that you have a familiar," she said. "I always envied the witches and wizards with their constant companions."

"Morgens must have a good relationship with animals, though, right? You're kind of woodsy."

"Woodsy?" Lacey echoed. "Not really. We're water spirits, so similar to nymphs. We have an affinity for water—lakes and rivers, that kind of thing. Not the ocean so much."

"Right. Woodsy water," I said.

Lacey laughed. "We don't have the same connection to animals as you have with your familiar. I'd love a talking cat in my life."

"I would've taken a cat, too, but I got a raccoon," I said.

Fitz polished off his drink. "A raccoon? I like it. Very feral." He gave me a hungry look and I wondered whether Florian came on this strong when he met a new woman. It was probably a numbers game—the more women you hit on, the more likely you were to score.

"Grandmother, Stone and I would like to give you our present," Avonne announced, "but it involves going to the front of the house."

"Only if you're up for it, Hattie," Stone added. He'd finally returned from his phone call on the lawn. "We can wait until later."

Hattie lowered her chair to the ground. "It's a present," she said. "Do I look like a moron to you? Of course, I'm up for it. When you get to be my age, there's no sense in waiting. You never know when it will be the last present you ever receive."

"Grandmother says what's on her mind," Fitz whispered. "We call her filterless."

Hattie held out her arm for assistance and Stone rushed

over to escort her. Everyone waited for them to enter the house first. We trailed behind them down the hallway and through the foyer. As they crossed the middle of the foyer, I heard a loud, creaking sound, followed by a snap. The chandelier dropped and I instinctively yanked out my wand to perform a freeze spell. Stone was faster. He grabbed Hattie by the shoulders and leaped aside as the chandelier came crashing down.

"*Glacio!*" I said. While I didn't save any lives, I managed to keep the pieces of crystal from flying in all directions. I looked over at Hattie and Stone to see them both shaking.

Avonne appeared visibly upset. She hurried over to wrap her arms around her husband and her grandmother.

Hattie brushed her aside. "No need to fuss. Everyone's fine." She glanced up at the empty place on the ceiling where the chandelier had been. "Sampson, I want to know which cleaner was the last one to touch that chandelier because she's fired." She narrowed her eyes at the butler. "I'll let you do the honors."

"Yes, mistress." Sampson bowed slightly before disappearing from the foyer.

"Let's get on with the show," Hattie said. She began hobbling across the foyer to the front door. "I don't want my birthday roast to get cold just to see some lame present I could've bought for myself if I'd truly wanted it."

To my surprise, no one reacted to Hattie's rude declaration. The family simply followed her out the front door as though she'd commented on the weather.

"What do you think, Grandmother?" Avonne asked.

I peered over a shoulder to glimpse—a purple and blue unicorn? "Wow," I breathed. I'd never seen a unicorn in bright colors before.

"Your favorite colors," Stone said proudly.

Now that Stone was in closer proximity, I noticed that his

loud shirt was also in purple and blue. Probably not a coincidence.

"I suppose that's better than last year's gift," Hattie said. She wagged a finger at Stone. "You're finally learning."

Stone's relief was evident. He escorted the elderly morgen down the steps to examine the unicorn up close while I took a few photos with my phone. Hattie stroked the beast's purple snout.

"She's a beauty, Grandmother," Fitz said. "Not as beautiful as you, of course." He gave Hattie a quick kiss on the cheek.

"Enough with the flattery," Hattie said, swatting at him. "The gods know you get enough out of me as it is."

Fitz slipped into the background without another word.

"I'll have Sampson bring the unicorn to the stables to join the others," Lacey offered.

"No, Sampson is busy with my party," Hattie said. "Have the gardener do it." She retreated into the house and everyone closed in behind her like lemmings. We skirted the frozen chandelier and assembled in the formal dining room. I knew I was supposed to make a note of all the place settings and accouterments—the types of things the readers of the society section would be interested in—but I had no idea what anything was called. I took more photos instead and decided to ask Simon to identify everything later. Aunt Hyacinth's butler would answer without judging my ignorance. That was his way.

Hattie sat at the head of the table, of course. To her left were Lacey, Avonne, and Stone. To her right sat Ella, Fitz, and me. Sampson appeared in the doorway. "Mrs. Ballywick will bring in the first course momentarily, mistress."

"Wine, Sampson?" Fitz asked, tapping his empty glass.

"And don't forget my special fizzlewick mead for the toast," Hattie said.

Sampson turned to the sideboard and popped the lid off a

decanter. He poured the reddish-purple liquid into a glass with the letter 'H' etched into it. He delivered the single glass on a tray and set it in front of Hattie. She removed the glass and inhaled the scent of the mead before sighing loudly.

Sampson proceeded to pour wine into the remaining glasses. Hattie waited until we each had a full glass before raising her own. "A toast to my two hundredth birthday. May you all live as long as I do and be as rich as I am, so that your family gives a minotaur shit about you."

Beside me, Fitz cleared his throat, clearly embarrassed. "To Hattie."

Everyone lifted their glasses and said, "To Hattie." No one sounded particularly enthused.

The birthday girl drank her mead with a speed usually reserved for frat boys at a keg party. I was gobsmacked that she wouldn't choose to savor the taste of the special drink she only allowed herself to enjoy once per year. Maybe there was something about reaching the age of two hundred that made one hasty.

We sat back in our seats and, as Hattie lowered herself down, she missed the chair and fell onto the floor. At least that was what I assumed happened. It was only when I saw Lacey's ashen face and Ella drop to the floor beside her that I realized something much worse had occurred.

"Help her!" Lacey cried. "I think she's having a heart attack."

"Aunt Hattie!" Ella cried.

We hovered over Hattie as she gripped her chest and her face turned a deep shade of purple that matched the mead.

Fitz kneeled beside her and tried to administer emergency life-saving techniques, but it was too late.

Hattie Rollins-Mahoney was dead.

CHAPTER THREE

"Why call the sheriff if Aunt Hattie had a heart attack?" Ella asked.

We sat in the formal living room, awaiting the arrival of Sheriff Nash and Deputy Bolan. No one wanted to sit in the dining room with Hattie's lifeless body.

"It's standard procedure, miss," Sampson said. "I've taken the liberty of calling the healer, too, as their office will most likely perform the autopsy. It's more efficient than waiting for the sheriff's office to arrange for transport."

Fitz pointed a finger at the butler. "Always thinking, Sampson," he said.

"Does there need to be an autopsy?" Ella asked. She seemed distressed. To be fair, everyone did, including me.

"Fair point," Fitz said. "I don't know that you need a cause of death for a two hundred-year-old morgen."

"I bet she was still in shock from the chandelier falling," Avonne said. "Her blood pressure was probably way up, but it didn't really hit her until she went to relax."

"That's plausible," Stone said. He sat beside his wife with his hand resting on her thigh.

Lacey glanced worriedly at the shared wall between the living and dining rooms. "I hate leaving her alone in there. It feels disrespectful."

"Look at it this way," Fitz said, "Grandmother won't give you a hard time about it now."

"Fitz, don't be horrible," Ella scolded him.

The doorbell rang and I waited to see whether the sheriff or the healer would arrive first.

Sheriff Granger Nash swaggered into the living room, ready for action. His brow lifted when he registered my presence. "One wealthy family not enough for you, Rose? Expanding your empire?"

"I'm here on assignment for the paper," I said.

He scratched his beard. "The paper heard about this before we did?"

I shook my head. "No, I was covering Hattie's birthday party for the society section. No one expected her to die." Or did they?

Deputy Bolan toddled in after him. The leprechaun nearly had a heart attack of his own when he spotted me in the room. "You can't be serious." He glanced at the sheriff. "I'd better keep my eye on you. The longer you two date, the more I worry you're going to end up in a body bag."

"You two are an item?" Fitz asked. I couldn't tell whether he was disappointed or surprised.

The sheriff gave a brief nod. "In the interest of full disclosure, Miss Rose and I are courting."

I pressed my lips together in an effort not to laugh. Who said courting? Then again, it was kind of adorable.

"Grandmother was two hundred years old," Fitz said, stepping forward. "It can hardly surprise anyone that she finally hit her limit."

"Be that as it may," the sheriff said, "we may as well take a look around. Once we get the autopsy report, we'll know for sure what we're dealing with."

"On that note, we'd like everyone to stay put for the time being," Deputy Bolan said. "We need to secure the area and then we'll be asking you some questions."

"If there's any staff in the house, we'll need a word with them, too," the sheriff added.

"I'll alert Mrs. Ballywick," Sampson said. "She's the housekeeper."

"No chef?" the sheriff inquired. "How about a gardener? That's a nice piece of property to keep orderly."

"No chef," Fitz said. "The gardener comes twice a week. He was here yesterday."

"Mr. Burroughs was here earlier today as well," Sampson said. "Your grandmother was unhappy with his work on the bushes in the southeast garden and requested that he return before the party to make the necessary improvements."

"And where's the deceased?" the sheriff asked.

"In the dining room," Lacey said, her voice cracking.

I raised my hand. "Um, sheriff? Do I need to stay, too?"

His eyes twinkled as his gaze rested on me. "No special treatment, Rose. Don't worry. I won't be long. I know how your bladder works."

He wasn't wrong. I'd be desperate for the bathroom before too long.

"Looks like there was an issue with the chandelier in the foyer," the deputy said. "Can anybody shed light on that?" He chuckled. "No pun intended."

"It fell earlier," Avonne said. "We were all going to the front of the house to see one of Grandmother's gifts when it came crashing down. If it weren't for my husband…." She trailed off. I knew what she intended to say—*Grandmother would still be alive*. Except she wasn't. His heroics had served no purpose.

25

Sheriff Nash scanned the group. "The chandelier came down on your grandmother?"

"We were all moving through the foyer at the same time, really," Stone said. "Hattie and I were leading the way. The chandelier came loose as we crossed beneath it. I managed to get us both to safety." His expression clouded over. "Not that it matters now."

"Hmm," the sheriff said. "Did you make a note of that, Deputy?"

"Sure did, boss."

The doorbell rang and Sampson returned a couple of minutes later with Cephas, one of the local druid healers. "This is not a resuscitation, I take it?"

"Sorry, no," the sheriff replied. "We'll be needing the autopsy report. Natural causes is likely, but there's a busted chandelier that suggests there might be more to it."

"That chandelier is more ancient than Grandmother," Avonne said. "It's not surprising that it finally came loose."

"And she was two hundred today," Fitz said. "You can't exactly complain when you make it that far."

"Depends on your species," the sheriff said. "Two hundred for a werewolf would be a miracle. If I were a vamp, I might be a tad disappointed."

Deputy Bolan snickered. "Everybody stay here while we secure the dining room and let Cephas get to work."

"Oh, crap-on-a-stick," I said.

The leprechaun eyed me. "Is there a problem, Ember?"

I looked uneasily from the deputy to the sheriff. "The butler may have already cleaned up the dining room."

Splotches of red appeared on Deputy Bolan's green face. He looked like he was morphing into an angry Christmas tree. "Let me get this straight—you leave dishes in the sink for days, but you let this guy clean everything out from under you? That's against your nature."

"How do you know I leave dishes in the sink?" I glared at the sheriff from across the room.

The sheriff's gaze shifted away from me and he began to whistle.

The deputy sighed loudly. "Once I'm done investigating the foyer, maybe you could do a spell that cleans up the mess, so no one gets a foot full of crystal?"

I saluted him. "I'm at your disposal, Deputy Bolan."

The leprechaun blew out an annoyed breath. "Sometimes I wish you were *in* my disposal," he muttered.

"What a lovely house," Cephas said, gazing at the expensive furnishings. "Not a bad place to end a long life, really."

The sheriff arched an eyebrow. "That all depends on how it ended."

"What do I buy for a house full of girls?" I asked. Florian and I were shopping in town after my release from the Rollins Estate. Although I was still a little shaken up after watching a stranger die in front of me, I had a daughter's monumental eleventh birthday party to focus on.

Florian smirked. "I can tell you my go-to purchases for a house full of girls…."

I grimaced. "Florian, they're ten and eleven years old."

"Hmm. In that case, I have no suggestions. You should've brought Linnea." He grabbed a demon mask from the shelf and put it on. "To be young again. I miss those days."

I stopped in the middle of the aisle and stared at his demonic face. "You have more money than Zeus. You have almost no responsibility. You're incredibly handsome and nauseatingly charming." I paused. "What exactly do you miss about your eleven-year-old self?"

Florian removed the mask and I saw his expression soften. "My dad was alive then."

"Oh." I felt awful. My cousin rarely displayed any genuine emotions and now I'd brought him close to tears in the toy aisle. Go me!

He set the mask back on the shelf. "No worries. Let's concentrate on that darling daughter of yours. She's not that keen on toys, is she?"

"No, but I need party bags for the other girls," I said. "I have no idea what a typical girl likes." Marley had never been typical for her age, so my frame of reference was completely skewed.

"You should have asked Bryn, actually," Florian said. "She's been eleven the most recently of all the Roses."

"Yes, but she'll give me that look of disdain that teenagers perfect so well whenever I suggest something," I said. "And Hudson will probably choose…whatever werewolf boys like."

Florian wiggled his eyebrows. "Werewolf girls."

I continued down the aisle and turned the corner. "I can't stop thinking about Hattie and her family. You should meet her grandson, Fitz. He's your non-magical counterpart."

"I probably have met him," Florian said. "Starry Hollow isn't that big. I just don't pay attention to my own gender unless they're supplying me with something I like."

I stood in front of an entire section of magical craft supplies. "This might work. Do girls like crafts?"

"Can't you ask the mothers from school that you befriended?" He hesitated, suddenly remembering how my brief entanglement with the Power Puff moms panned out. The short answer was: not fabulous.

"I'm better off figuring this out on my own," I said.

"I feel like that was your way of life in New Jersey," Florian said. "Starry Hollow should be an improvement. Don't operate in a vacuum when you have resources available to you." He paused. "Not me, of course. I'm not remotely a resource for you under these circumstances."

"You're a big help, Florian. Don't sell yourself short." I began to fill my basket with magical yarn that changed colors depending on the color it was adjacent to. Chameleon Crochet.

"Are you going to get Marley anything magic related for her present?" Florian asked.

"Definitely not," I said. "What if she doesn't come into her magic? She'd be devastated to open a starter wand and not be able to use it."

"I guess that would be upsetting." Florian grabbed a selection of crochet hooks and patterns and chucked them into the basket. "She doesn't have any vampire friends coming over, does she? These might be hazardous if someone draws blood."

"There is one vampire," I said. I contemplated my potential purchases. "I don't need a midnight tragedy during our first sleepover."

"Speaking of first sleepovers…."

I rolled my eyes. "Oh, boy. Why do I already know where this is going?"

"Whenever you want to get it on with your big, bad wolf, just send Marley over to me or Linnea…even Aster, as long as the twins won't scar her."

I turned away from him and focused on the crafts. "I'll bear that in mind."

"You should be enjoying yourself, Ember," he said. "You've got a guy who's totally into you. He's the sheriff, so he's got that sexy swagger and the whole air of authority thing going on."

I raised an eyebrow. "Sounds like *you* might want a sleepover with the sheriff."

"You know my gender preference," he replied. "I'm only looking out for your interests."

"And I appreciate that," I said. "You're a good cousin."

"I know you'd do the same for me," he said, "mainly because you have."

"No second thoughts about Delphine?" I asked. He'd briefly dated Delphine Winter, the town librarian, but they'd recently parted as friends.

"None," he said. "I'm not ready to settle down, no matter how much my mother wants it to happen."

I selected a few more items from the craft aisle, including felt and blank masks, and paid at the register. "What if I'm not ready to settle down?" I asked. "I don't know that I should be encouraging sleepovers if I can't fully commit."

Florian took the bag from my arms and opened the door of the shop. Despite his womanizing behavior, he was still a gentleman in many ways.

"You are ready, Ember," he said. "You've already been through a lot in your life at a young age. You're just afraid and it's perfectly understandable."

"What's Rose understandably afraid of?" Sheriff Nash appeared on the pavement in front of us.

"Ghosts," I said quickly. My heart began to beat rapidly. "The ones that move things." I snapped my fingers. "Poltergeists."

The sheriff cocked his head. "I see. Glad I ran into you. I have the results from Hattie's autopsy."

"That was fast," I said.

"I asked Cephas to put a rush on it," he said. "I had a feeling we weren't looking at natural causes."

"So it wasn't a heart attack?" I asked.

"Oh, it was a heart attack, but not a naturally occurring one," he replied.

I squinted. "So not because of the falling chandelier or stress of the party?"

"No," he replied. "We found a substance in her system

called celeritas. An accelerant that's used in speed potions, as well as a lot of calorie burning potions."

"Was she taking any potions?" I asked. It seemed feasible that a two hundred-year-old woman would be taking at least a couple of them.

"Not anything with celeritas, according to her butler or housekeeper," the sheriff said.

"How do you think it got into her system?" I asked.

He shrugged. "Based on the information we have, it looks like someone tampered with her special mead. It's the one item that would've masked the taste and celeritas is pretty fast-acting, especially in someone Hattie's age. Anyway, I got a list of everything she ate and drank that day from Sampson, just to make sure we're not missing anything. That butler's a detailed fella."

"Like Simon," I said, glancing at Florian.

"You have to be detail-oriented when you work for a demanding head of household," Florian said. "You need thick skin, too."

"What are your next steps?" I asked the sheriff.

"Talk to everyone at the party again and the rest of her staff," he replied. "Find out who stands to inherit the estate so we can assess motives. That sort of thing. You know the drill, Rose."

"My society article has now been moved to the front page," I said. "Count me in for questioning."

"You were there," the sheriff said. "I need to question *you* again." He winked. "Maybe I could do that part somewhere nice and quiet where we can really talk."

"Like her bedroom?" Florian offered.

I elbowed my cousin in the ribs and he nearly dropped the bag of crafts.

The sheriff struggled to keep a straight face. "A bedroom

probably isn't the most professional of places for an interrogation."

"Oh? Now it's an interrogation?" I asked. "That sounds
more intense. I thought it was a few questions."

A smile tugged at his lips. "It's always more intense when
it's you and me, Rose."

Florian took a big step forward. "On that intimate note,
I'll meet you at the car, Ember."

Sheriff Nash chuckled. "Too hot for you to handle,
Florian?"

My cousin didn't answer. He strode to the car, leaving me
alone with my sort-of boyfriend.

"How about it, Rose?" he asked, edging closer. "Dinner
tonight?"

"I'll see if Mrs. Babcock can make dinner for Marley," I
said. My pulse quickened as he leaned down to kiss my
cheek.

"Sounds like a date." He patted his stomach. "I'll go easy
on lunch, so as not to ruin my appetite for you...I mean, for
dinner."

The gesture triggered a memory from Hattie's party.
"Lacey," I said. "Hattie's eldest grandchild."

"What about her?"

"She was trying to lose weight," I said. "She mentioned a
calorie burning potion. We should talk to her before we go to
dinner."

The sheriff gave me an admiring look. "I can always count
on you to worm your way into an investigation."

"Maybe I just like spending time with you," I said.

"Ha! A bald-faced lie," he said, "but I'll take it." He kissed
me again, this time full on the lips. "I'll pick you up at six so
we have time to swing by Lacey's before dinner."

I stood on the pavement, my whole body energized by the
kiss. "I'll be ready."

CHAPTER FOUR

LACEY'S modest house was so unlike Hattie's sprawling estate, it was hard to believe the occupants were related. Although Linnea and Aster's houses weren't comparable to Thornhold, they both reflected a certain elegance and style that had clearly been passed down by their mother. I couldn't say the same for Lacey.

"Are you sure this is it?" I asked the sheriff, as we stood on the doorstep. The shutters were in desperate need of a new coat of paint and the garden was neglected to the point where I couldn't discern the weeds from the flowers. And yet Lacey had seemed so polished at the birthday party. The pains she took with her appearance didn't seem to extend to the appearance of her home.

Lacey jerked the door open. Her hair was pulled up in a messy bun and she looked far more haggard than her appearance at the party. Apparently, she'd made an effort for her grandmother's birthday.

"Sheriff?" Lacey's gaze shifted to me. "You always take your dates on official business?"

"I'm covering Hattie's story for the paper," I said. "The sheriff is kind enough to let me accompany him."

"I'll bet." Lacey stood aside and ushered us inside. "I don't suppose this is good news." She headed into the kitchen of the open-plan first floor.

"Afraid not," the sheriff said. "The autopsy report shows that your grandmother suffered a heart attack."

Lacey squinted. "Isn't that what we thought?"

"If it had been the result of natural causes, then yes," the sheriff replied. "Unfortunately, the attack appears to have been brought on by a potion in her system. Based on the evidence, we believe that the potion was administered via Hattie's glass of fizzlewick mead."

Lacey balked. "Great Bel! Not the mead. How is that even possible? No one was allowed to touch it."

"That's what we're trying to figure out," Sheriff Nash said. "Any information you can share would be helpful."

Lacey moved like a zombie to stand behind the kitchen counter. She seemed to be in shock. "Grandmother was really murdered?"

"Apparently so," the sheriff said.

Lacey grabbed a sponge and wiped down one end of the counter. I could tell she was operating on autopilot. "The potion in the mead caused her heart attack?"

"That's right." I noticed that the sheriff didn't share the type of potion, nor did Lacey ask. "It caused her heart to work overtime, which resulted in her death. A woman Hattie's age couldn't tolerate it."

Lacey began emptying debris from the lunchboxes on the counter. "Are you sure it wasn't a potion she was taking herself? You should ask Sampson or Mrs. Ballywick."

"I already have," the sheriff said. "It wasn't one of her usual supplements and there was no sign of it in the house."

Lacey scrubbed the piping on the interior of the lunchbox. "I hate seeing the remnants of all their good snacks," she said absently. "Makes my diet that much harder."

"How long have you been trying to lose weight?" I asked.

She offered a begrudging smile. "It seems like I've been trying to move the same ten pounds for the past year. The kids' snacks don't help. I can't resist them."

"I didn't even realize you had kids until now," I said. "Why weren't they at the party?"

"Grandmother doesn't…didn't like children to be present at parties," Lacey said. "She said they took the attention away from her. Avonne has children, too. They were with a nanny."

"How old are your children?" Judging from the lunchboxes, they were still fairly young.

"My daughter is twelve and my son is ten," she replied. "They spent the weekend with their father since he wasn't invited to the party either." She sighed. "At least I was able to spend the night before the party with Grandmother, especially in light of the outcome. It was nice to be just the two of us for a change. Every event is always such a gathering with my family. It's exhausting at times, all the pretending to get along." She blew a raspberry.

"You and the father of your kids…You're not together anymore?" the sheriff asked.

She shook her head and a few dark tendrils fell loose. "Weston and I were doomed from the start. Grandmother never approved of our relationship. She made it difficult for us to stay together, always making a fuss over him being a shifter. Adds a lot of stress to a marriage, when the family… well, when a key family member disapproves."

"Hattie did that?" I asked. I couldn't imagine someone trying to exert so much control…Wait a hot minute. Of course I could—and her name was Hyacinth Rose-Muldoon.

Lacey moved on from the lunchboxes to the dirty dishes

35

in the sink. "After our parents died, Grandmother became more tyrannical about our choices. I'm the oldest so, naturally, I bore the brunt of her demands."

"I hate to ask an intrusive question…." I began.

"But hey, you're a journalist, right?" Lacey managed a smile. "My parents died in a yachting accident years ago."

"I'm sorry," I said. "I lost my parents, too. I know it's hard."

"It was a long time ago." She paused for a thoughtful moment. "Please excuse my manners. Can I offer you anything? Granola bar? Ale?"

"We're good, thanks," the sheriff said.

Lacey dropped the dirty dishes into what looked like a hole in the countertop. I leaned forward for a better view. "What are you doing?"

She looked at me. "Loading the dishwasher. What do you think?"

"You're dropping them into a hole."

The sheriff chuckled. "You've never seen one like that, Rose? We need to get you out of the house more often."

"They're designed by elves," Lacey explained. "You drop in your dirty dishes and they come out the end completely clean." She walked to the end of the counter and patted the side that I couldn't see. "There's also a spell for stacking imbued in the design as well, so everything piles up or lines up as needed."

"How about that?" I asked, amazed.

"Elves, nymphs, morgens… all other non-users of magic have to find a way to be inventive," Lacey said. She smiled at the sheriff. "You know what I mean, don't you?"

He inclined his head. "I certainly do."

"Well, I've lived most of my life without magic," I said, "so that's still how I tend to function. I'm learning, though."

Lacey rested her elbows on the countertop. "If I had magic, life would be so much easier."

"Everyone says that, but I don't know that it's true," I said.

"Good point," Lacey said. "At least I would've been higher in the social hierarchy. Magic users are always more revered."

"That's definitely not true," I said. "I've seen some of the pixies and fairies in this town. Revered is not the word I'd use."

"Then again, Grandmother hated that Weston wasn't a 'better' species, so there's always a reason to look down on someone else. She considered shifters to be nothing more than dirty animals." She glanced at the sheriff. "No offense, Sheriff Nash. I obviously don't feel that way or I wouldn't have married one."

Although the sheriff didn't react, I knew the sentiment bothered him. How could it not?

"Morgens aren't that common in this area, are they?" I asked. I didn't know much about them and I'd learned a lot about different species since my arrival in Starry Hollow.

"No, not at all. It's one of the main reasons Grandmother felt so strongly about preserving the bloodline, to the extent possible, since morgens can only be female. She wanted Fitz to marry a morgen and have a bunch of daughters. With Fitz being a water nymph, the girls would definitely be morgens."

I thought of Aunt Hyacinth's determination to marry Florian off to a witch. "Your grandmother must have objected before your wedding. Why be so difficult once you'd gone through with it? Why not accept it?"

"Because she was stubborn and racist. She threatened to write me out of the will." Lacey splayed her hands on the countertop. "I didn't believe her. Like I said, I was the eldest. I thought I was untouchable." She laughed bitterly. "Grandmother sure showed me. Now I'm a single mother with very little money and ten extra pounds that keep the men away."

I wasn't convinced the ten extra pounds were the problem, but I kept my mouth shut.

"You said you had an evening alone with Hattie the night before the party," the sheriff began. "What did the two of you do?"

Lacey hugged herself and smiled. "We played a card game and then I listened while she told some of her favorite childhood stories. We each had a glass of Goddess Bounty before bed. I liked her best in these quiet moments. She didn't talk down to me or boss me around. I got to see her softer side one last time."

"Sounds like a blessing," I said.

"Where did you sleep that night?" the sheriff asked.

"In the Sunflower Suite," Lacey said. "It was my room at the estate when I was younger. So bright and cheerful." Her voice grew wistful. "I miss it there."

"Did you see her at breakfast?" I asked.

"No, Avonne had breakfast alone with her while I went to yoga with Iris Sandstone," Lacey said. "You should be able to confirm that easily enough, given that she's the High Priestess of your coven." She gave me a pointed look. "I've been skipping breakfast as part of my diet plan. Drinking my meal replacement potion instead. It's supposed to keep me feeling full for hours afterward."

"Could I have the name of that potion?" the sheriff asked.

Lacey tapped her fingernails on the countertop. "I'll have to check. I've been through so many diet products recently. It's hard to keep track."

"You must've taken some this morning," the sheriff said. "Where do you keep the bottle?"

"In the bathroom," she said. "I drink it right before I brush my teeth."

The sheriff offered a patient smile. "I can wait right here while you get it. I'm not in a hurry."

Lacey's eyes rounded. "Oh. Okay. I'll look now." I couldn't tell whether she was stalling or just dim.

The moment Lacey left the room, the sheriff pinched my bottom. "Hey!" I said, swatting his hand away. "We're here on professional business."

He grinned. "I know, but you were sticking it out at just the right angle. I couldn't resist."

"I wasn't sticking out my butt," I said, indignant. "That's weird."

He bumped me with his hip. "You're weird, so it fits."

Lacey returned with a deep blue bottle in her hand and I immediately straightened. "Here it is. Not sure how effective it is since I haven't been taking it very long." The label read— Muffin Top Pop.

"About how long would you say?" the sheriff asked.

She looked thoughtful. "This one? Probably four days. I'm not sure why you need it, though. There's no way Grandmother was taking any diet potions. She was as thin as a string bean under those billowy kaftans."

"Would you mind if I took this bottle?" the sheriff asked. "You have more, right?"

Lacey seemed put out. "I guess so. They're not cheap, though."

The sheriff plucked the bottle from her hand. "Thanks, I appreciate it. One last question. Have you ever been in the mead cellar?" the sheriff asked.

Lacey grimaced. "Gods, no. Grandmother was always very territorial about it. Fitz lives down there and I think he's only managed one peek in there."

"Fitz? That's your brother?" the sheriff asked.

"Yes, he lives on the lower level of the estate," Lacey said.

"He's the grandson and heir, you know. He gets to do what he wants, unlike me."

"Sounds familiar, doesn't it, Rose?" the sheriff asked.

"If Florian lived next to a mead cellar, I guarantee you that the entire stock would be gone by now," I said.

Lacey pulled the pins out of her messy bun and her hair fell loose down her shoulders. "It wouldn't surprise me if the mead cellar is empty the next time I go over to the estate. Fitz has expensive taste and no scruples. He wouldn't bother to wait for the reading of the will."

"Expensive taste and no scruples, huh?" Sheriff Nash asked. "Sounds like the kind of guy I should be talking to. We appreciate your time, Lacey. I'll be in touch."

She gave a defeated wave. "If you know any single shifters, Sheriff Nash, I'm not picky."

"Maybe that's your problem," I said.

Lacey glared at me. "You try being a single mother on a budget while the rest of your family lives in luxury. It isn't easy."

Sheriff Nash opened his mouth to speak and I silenced him with a look. I didn't need him to defend me.

"Maybe you're back in the will because you split up with Weston," I said. "That would help your situation."

Lacey smiled. "I've been trying not to get my hopes up. Grandmother never said whether she wrote me back in. That was the hope, but I didn't dare ask. She was spiteful enough to write me out again, just for questioning it."

"She sounds like she was a delightful woman," I said. As delightful as a chainsaw across the back of my legs.

Lacey's expression appeared pained. "I know it seems strange in light of everything I said, but she'll be sorely missed."

I gave her arm a squeeze. "That's how it always is with family, Lacey."

The sheriff and I left Lacey's house and headed to dinner.

"Do you know Weston?" I asked.

"No, he's not a werewolf," the sheriff said. "Different kind of shifter."

I bit my lip. "Do you think she was flirting with you?" I moved my index finger and thumb an inch apart. "Maybe a smidge?"

"If she were, then she was only doing it because she doesn't want to be considered a suspect. Happens a lot."

"Because she's guilty?"

"I don't know that yet. We've got the potion." He patted his pocket. "We've also got her unsupervised access to the house the night before, and her resentment over Weston."

Despite all that, Lacey didn't *seem* guilty. "I don't know. If she were written back into the will…."

"Then all the more reason to kill her now," the sheriff interjected. "She'd get her revenge and her money at the same time."

"She's pretty, but her attitude is kind of sour. That's a turn-off." I looked at him for confirmation. "Right?"

The sheriff reached for my hand. "I like this side of you, Rose. I should tell folks we're courting more often."

"If she was flirting, then it was rude," I said. "You'd made it clear that we were a couple."

"She desires male attention," the sheriff said. "That much was clear."

"I wonder if she'll get back together with Weston now that Hattie is out of the picture." Although Weston sounded as bad as Wyatt with the philandering streak. Maybe Lacey didn't want him back.

"If she feels desperate enough, she might," the sheriff said. "I bet Hattie left her high and dry in that will, even though Lacey divorced him. And I'll check with Iris Sandstone about the yoga, but I believe her. Even if she's guilty, she could've slipped the potion into that mead the night before. No one would be the wiser."

"We should pay a visit to Fitz," I said. "He kept insisting that her age was the culprit, like he needed to convince everyone."

"You're reading my mind, Rose," he said. "That guy has motive and opportunity written all over him." He opened the passenger door for me. "Come to think of it, you should go see Fitz."

I stared at him. "I just said that."

"You said 'we.' I think you should go on your own," he said. "A guy like that is much more likely to blather on and reveal precious secrets if he thinks he has a chance with you."

I arched an eyebrow. "Is that so? I don't think I've heard many of your secrets, Sheriff Nash."

"That's because I'm an open book, Rose." He spread his arms wide. "What you see is what you get."

That was the truth. I took the opportunity to run my fingers through his thick hair. It felt nice.

The sheriff studied me closely. "Rose, you got something on your mind?"

I inhaled deeply. "I've been thinking," I began.

He took a few steps backward. "Whoa. Should I be concerned?"

"Not if you're interested in the next step in our relationship."

He broke into a broad grin. "Next step, huh? And what does that entail?"

"I'd rather show you than tell you," I replied.

He slipped an arm around my waist. "I'm liking this conversation more and more, Rose. Keep talking."

"I've been inspired by Marley's upcoming sleepover," I said, remembering my conversation with Florian.

He frowned. "A kid's birthday party? Okay, now my mind is wandering in a less interesting direction."

I waved my hands. "No, no. Stay on track. Your instincts were right."

He wiped his forehead. "Phew. Had me worried there for a nanosecond."

"Florian suggested that it's time to progress. Maybe the weekend after Marley's party, you could come over for dinner and then...stay?"

The werewolf stroked his chin. "I'm willing to overlook the fact that you have oddly intimate conversations with your male cousin, but only because the offer you've made is making me a little dizzy."

I peered at him. "Good dizzy?"

He pulled me against his chest and kissed me hard. "The best kind of dizzy."

CHAPTER FIVE

I SMOOTHED the frizz from my hair and adjusted the hem of my skirt before ringing the bell at the Rollins Manor. I didn't want to go too far with the sheriff's suggestion, but I agreed that Fitz seemed like the kind of guy I could weasel information out of with a tight blouse and a few well-chosen compliments. I wouldn't even need to ply him with alcohol.

Like Florian, Fitz had his own entrance to his bachelor pad on the lower level of the house, which made it easy for his conquests to come and go sight unseen. I rang the bell and waited, knowing that Sampson wouldn't be trekking to this side of the house to answer Fitz's door. He'd likely been forbidden from doing so.

After a few minutes, the door opened and Fitz stood on the landing, looking every inch the attractive male heir that he was. It was no small wonder that the water nymph hadn't settled down. The combination of looks and money had to be an aphrodisiac that few women could resist.

Fitz leaned his well-defined bicep against the doorjamb. "Well, hello there, Miss Rose. I didn't expect to see you again so soon."

"I'm still working on my article for *Vox Populi* and I had a few questions about your grandmother," I said. "Would you mind if I came in?"

Fitz smirked the way he probably did whenever a lamb entered his slaughterhouse. "Don't mind at all. Watch your step. They're narrow down here."

I followed him down to his man cave. It wasn't as impressive as Florian's, but it definitely reeked of wealth and privilege. The unicorn head mounted on the wall nearly made my head explode.

"Please tell me that's not real," I said, pointing to the unicorn.

"It isn't…anymore," he replied. "Drink? I have plenty of alcohol. I'm well-stocked for all the girly cocktails." He wiggled his eyebrows. "Though you don't strike me as the girly cocktail type." He studied me carefully. "You're as happy with an ale as anything else."

"An ale will be fine," I replied. Best to keep my nausea at bay. I had a feeling the more I got to know Fitz, the more repulsive he'd become. I watched as he poured to make sure he didn't slip anything into my drink. Assuming he was willing to poison his own grandmother, he was capable of anything.

He handed me a glass and poured one for himself. "Salut," he said, and tapped his glass against mine.

"Salut." I took a sip. "I'm sorry about your grandmother, Fitz. You must still be reeling from the shock."

"Two hundred and you think I'm shocked?" He shrugged. "I've been preparing for this day for a long time now."

My brow lifted. "You have?" I carefully surveyed the room, looking for any sign of potions or paraphernalia that could have contributed to Hattie's death. I saw golf clubs, fishing rods, and a surfboard. Fitz certainly had a lot of…stuff.

"Why don't we make ourselves comfortable?" he said, leading me to the plush sofa. He took up residence in the middle of the cushion, forcing me into close proximity.

"Your place is pretty cool," I said. "It was nice of Hattie to let you live here."

"I'm the heir," he replied. "It's to be expected."

"So does that mean you'll be inheriting the house?" I asked.

"No, but that's another story," he said. Notably, he didn't seem too bothered about it. "I get to stay here and I expect to get a large sum of money, and that's all I care about."

"Were you close to Hattie?" I asked. "I imagine you must've been, living in such close quarters."

He laughed. "Maybe you haven't noticed, but it's an enormous house. I'd hardly call them close quarters."

"Well, you know what I mean. You basically live in the same house, unlike everyone else in the family."

He drank more ale. "I didn't see her much. I tended to avoid her. It got tiring to hear her bang on about how I needed to marry a morgen." He grinned at me. "She would've approved of you, though, if push came to shove. A descendant of the One True Witch?" He eyed me with a wolfish grin. "Definitely."

"Sounds like your grandmother had very vocal opinions about your personal life," I said. "You seem like such a strong and independent guy. That must've seriously annoyed you."

"Oh, I'm strong," he said, openly enjoying the flattery. "You should see how many pints I can lift at once." He laughed. "Who am I kidding? They're all empty so quickly." He shifted closer to me. "So how serious are you and the sheriff? You should consider upgrading. I mean, the guy makes a public servant's salary. He can't possibly be marriage material for a witch of your caliber."

I stood abruptly before my fist betrayed me and

punched him in his smug face. It seemed that Hattie's preju-
dices had rubbed off on her entitled grandson. Not that it
came as a surprise. I pretended to show an interest in his
decor so as not to let my anger build. I swiveled away from
the repulsive unicorn head and focused on other parts of
the room.

"You have such eclectic taste," I said. For most of the
items, I had no clue what I was viewing. There was a selection of masks on the wall that seemed suggestive of different
animals.

"Those are tribal masks," Fitz said, moving to stand beside
me. His breath reeked of ale and I wondered how many he'd
imbibed before my arrival. Breakfast of champions, it
seemed.

"I feel an energy around them," I said. It was strange, like
a prickling sensation.

Fitz clapped his hands together. "That's awesome. Your
magic must be really strong. I've never had anyone here who
could detect it."

"So they're magical tribal masks?" I queried.

"You bet," he replied. "The tribe members used to put
them on and turn into whatever animal was displayed on the
mask. It was part of a ritual."

"Wow," I breathed. That actually sounded cool. I thought
of the cute craft masks I bought for Marley's party and
wondered whether there was a way I could make them more
interesting.

"They were destined for a museum," Fitz continued, "but I
managed to persuade the owner to sell them to me instead. I
like having things no one else does."

"Now you sound like Hattie and her fizzlewick mead," I
said, trying to lead the conversation back to the murder. "I
suppose you've already broken into her stash."

"I haven't, in fact," he replied. "Deputy Bolan warned me

not to touch anything out of the ordinary in the house or I could be tampering with evidence."

"That makes sense," I said.

"I don't see why the mead matters," he said. "It's in the cellar where no one's allowed to go."

Ah, so the leprechaun didn't divulge the means of delivery of the fatal potion. If this family convened as often as mine, they'd all know the details by now. Aunt Hyacinth would have made sure of it. Or maybe not, since in the comparable scenario, she'd be the murder victim. I shivered at the thought.

"Are you chilly?" Fitz asked. He draped an arm along my shoulders. "I can think of a few ways to keep you warm."

My instinct was to shake his arm away, but something across the room caught my eye, so I decided to let it stay put. "Looks like you have an effective tool right there." I pointed to the collection of items stashed in the corner of the room. "Is that a blowtorch?"

His gaze alighted on the pile of metal objects and he laughed. "You can tell how often I tidy up this place. Those are from ages ago, back when I used to rail against Grandmother's authority."

I took the opportunity to examine them more closely. "How did you use them?" Not only was there a blowtorch, but also a drill and a chisel.

He picked up the chisel and inspected it, blowing off the dust in the process. "If memory serves, these are from when my buddy and I got wasted and tried to bust through a wall into the mead cellar."

I held up a finger. "A-ha! I knew you wouldn't be able to stand being kept out of there."

Fitz grinned and set down the item. "I lost my interest in the mead when I became old enough to drink all over town and leave tabs in my grandmother's name. Her accountant takes care of my bills. It's nice." He tilted his head. "Would be even nicer to share that with a special someone."

"I would think the accounts will be frozen until your grandmother's death is fully investigated."

He scowled. "Good point. I hadn't thought of that. Bummer."

"Where's the key to the cellar now?" I asked. "Any idea?"

"There are two," Fitz said. "Grandmother wore one on a chain around her neck and Sampson has the other one. I'm not sure if we sent her out to sea wearing it. I didn't take a close look before the send-off."

"A water burial?" I asked.

"Morgens always do water burials. She would've preferred a lake, but the ocean's right there," Fitz said.

"Did Sampson ever go down to the cellar to clean or anything?" I asked.

"Not that I know of," Fitz said, "though he would've been the one to bring up the glass of mead for Grandmother's annual toast."

"She trusted Sampson that much that he had his own key?" I asked.

Fitz gave a firm nod. "She relied heavily on Sampson to do her bidding. I don't know how he tolerated her, quite frankly. She was as demanding as they come."

"Demanding enough that he'd want her gone?" I asked.

Fitz appeared surprised by my suggestion. "I hadn't considered that the butler would've done it. I suppose a lifetime of servitude could turn anyone violent."

"He would've had access to the chandelier, too," I said.

Fitz gave me an appreciative glance. "You're very smart. I like smart women." He threw his head back and laughed. "Who am I kidding? I like all women."

Ugh. Fitz was so much worse than Florian. The wizard had a soft and gentlemanly side that Fitz clearly lacked.

"Thanks for your time," I said, easing away from him. "I appreciate it."

"You're going?" He seemed disappointed. "I thought I could show you the rest of my place. You should see the artwork on my bedroom ceiling."

Gross. "Another time. I have a magic lesson that I can't be late for. I have a Hattie of my own, you see. She's also very demanding."

Fitz nodded solemnly. "I totally understand. May the wind be at your back."

The wind was at my back *and* my front. My hair whipped itself into a frenzy while I stood with Wren Stanton-Summer, Master-of-Incantation and wizard extraordinaire, on the clifftop overlooking Fairy Cove.

"I thought we'd work on glamours today," the handsome wizard said.

"I picture glamours as more of an indoor activity," I said.

"You can picture them however you like, but I'm in charge and we're having this lesson in the great outdoors." He made a big show of inhaling the fresh air.

I eyed him suspiciously. "You keep insisting on having lessons outside. You hate my cottage, don't you?"

Wren averted his gaze. "I don't know what you mean."

I pointed at him like a child. "Ha! I knew it. Admit it, Wren. You don't like being inside my cottage." My hands flew to my hips. "What's the issue? Not tidy enough for you? Smells like the enticing aroma of dog food and wet raccoon fur?" Gee, now that I said it out loud, it was amazing that *I* could stomach being inside my cottage.

Wren took a deep breath. "It's your dog, okay? I'm not a huge fan of that creature you live with."

My eyes nearly bugged out of my head. "PP3? Are you

serious?" The Yorkshire terrier was the most adorable, harmless dog in the history of dogs.

Wren turned toward the Whitethorn in the distance, clearly embarrassed. "Listen, I don't want to make a thing about it, but the dog gets under my skin. The way he looks at me. He's…creepy."

My laughter reverberated. "Creepy? Prescott Peabody III is many things, Wren, but creepy is not one of them."

Wren threw out his arms in frustration. "You asked me for the reason and I've decided to be honest. Don't make me regret it."

I didn't know what to say. I could understand a shifter or some other paranormal having an issue with PP3, but a strapping wizard like Wren? Complete shock.

"What if I could learn a glamour spell that made PP3 look like something more tolerable?" I suggested.

"I was planning to focus on glamouring your hair, but that's a good plan, too."

My hands instinctively touched my head. "What's wrong with my hair?" It was a pointless question. I knew exactly what was wrong with my hair. We were standing on a clifftop, enjoying a strong sea breeze. Just because it felt good, though, didn't mean it made me look good. I had no illusions about the frizz factor. The windswept look might work for some ladies, but I wasn't one of them. I looked like someone had caught me in a fishing net, and then dragged me along the surf for a mile before reeling me in. In the middle of a Category 5 hurricane.

Wren pressed his lips together. "We'll start with your idea." He surveyed the area for a PP3 stand-in. He was just about to reach for a sizable log when Raoul emerged from the trees.

"Well, what do you know?" Wren said. "A volunteer."

Raoul looked at me, his dark eyes glinting with suspicion. *What does he mean?*

"I need someone to practice glamour spells on," I said. "You're ideal."

Raoul waved his paws in front of him. *No, no, no. I'm a raccoon, not a guinea pig.*

Oh, come on. Don't be a spoilsport. I won't embarrass you.

Why should today be any different? Raoul grumbled.

I glared at him. *What if I bought pizza for dinner?*

And what would you and Marley have?

Fine, I huffed. *One large pizza for Raoul.*

With all the toppings, he added.

I shot him a quick look. "All?"

"Are you two negotiating?" Wren asked. "Don't you know not to negotiate with terrorists, Ember?"

"He's a bandit, not a terrorist. Don't let the mask fool you."

Raoul shook my hand. *Deal. Let's go, caster. Show me what you've got.*

I rolled my eyes. "Wren, whatever illusion I cast, can it involve muting him?"

A smile tugged at the corners of Wren's mouth. "Sure thing."

I looked from Wren to my familiar. "So what would you prefer to see when you walk in my house, Wren? A mermaid on the sofa probably won't cut it. She'll be gasping for water."

Wren shook his head. "I don't know why you think I have a thing for mermaids."

"Because you have a p...Because you're a dude."

The wizard glanced at the water beyond the cliff. "They have a certain appeal, I'll admit, but I'd like to settle down with a nice witch."

"What is it with wanting to stay within the coven?" I asked. "Why does it matter?"

Wren shrugged. "It's not a mandate. If I fall in love with someone and she happens to be a nymph or a fairy, I won't reject her. I just like the idea of everyone in my family being a part of the coven and having the same traditions. I guess it's kind of old-fashioned."

I felt myself softening. "Actually, Wren, it sounds really nice. I've just been hearing a lot of elitist remarks recently. I mean, I guess it's easy for me to say witches aren't superior because I am one, but I truly believe that." It seemed akin to wealthy people claiming that money isn't everything—it sure can seem that way when you don't have enough of it.

This wizard is a keeper, Ember. I'm telling you, if you ever get tired of that furball, you've got a prospect right here. Plus, you get that whole teacher-student vibe. Sexy. He began gyrating in a circle and singing *boom-chicka-bow-wow.*

I tried to ignore him and focus on the lesson. "How about a turtle? You don't want to date them. They don't talk, they're harmless, and they fit on my sofa."

Wren chuckled. "A turtle it is then. Wand at the ready, Ember."

I produced my wand and twirled it for good measure. "Armed and dangerous, captain."

He scrutinized me. "You do remember you're glamouring a raccoon to look like a turtle, right?"

I winked at Raoul. "Yep. A turtle. Hairless and with a shell. Got it."

Raoul appeared visibly ill. *I'm starting to regret my decision.*

"All the toppings," I reminded him.

He puffed out his chest. *Do your worst.*

Wren aimed his wand. "I'll demonstrate. Focus your will and picture Raoul as a tortoise."

"We agreed on turtle," I said.

Wren shot me a quizzical look. "What's the difference?"

I shrugged. "I don't know. You'd have to ask Marley."

Wren took aim again. "Focus your will and picture Raoul as a *turtle*. Then say *incanto testudo graeca*." Green light streaked from the tip of his wand. When I glanced at Raoul, a turtle blinked back at me.

"Very cool," I said. "It's still Raoul, though, right?"

"Yes, it's only an illusion," Wren replied.

"How long does it last?" I asked. I could already think of a number of ways this type of enchantment could be useful.

"If you don't add a time element, it wears off in a matter of minutes," Wren said. "I'll get rid of the glamour and then you can practice." He pointed his wand at the turtle and said, "*Restauro*."

Raoul replaced the turtle. *How'd I look as a turtle? Did my butt look big?*

You had a shell, not a butt.

Yeah, I guess the shell covers the fat butt.

I'm pretty sure turtles are skinny, I said.

Make sure I'm an astute turtle, he said. *I don't want to have that slow expression a lot of them wear. It doesn't fit with my brand.*

I laughed. *Your brand? You're a raccoon. You don't have a brand.*

Raoul folded his arms. *I do, too, have a brand. Sassy and sophisticated.*

I barked a short laugh. "Sophisticated? I don't think so. Your idea of a gourmet meal is the dumpster behind the French restaurant."

That's entirely sensible, mademoiselle, he replied, sticking his nose in the air.

I shook my head and aimed my wand. "*Incanto testuda.*" I peered down to see a lute on the ground. "Um, I think I may have gone astray somewhere."

Wren chuckled. "You think? Musical instruments aren't a

bad glamour, though. I wouldn't mind seeing a lute on your sofa. The only problem is I may decide to strum it."

"Oops. I guess I didn't focus my will," I said.

"You also didn't use the right phrase," Wren said.

I looked at him agape. "Then why didn't you stop me?"

He grinned. "I thought it would be fun to see what happened."

"You're a sadist."

"It doesn't hurt him," Wren said. "He feels the same. He just looks different to us." He winked. "Plus, he can't talk if he's an instrument, right? A win-win."

"Let me have another go," I said. This time, I made sure to focus my will and picture a turtle. *"Incanto testudo graeca."*

A sigh of relief escaped me when I saw the turtle reappear. "Excellent work, Ember," Wren said. "Now the restoration spell."

"Can't I leave him like this until it wears off?" I asked. "You said it wouldn't be long." I looked admiringly at my handiwork. "I'm envisioning all sorts of fun at Marley's sleepover party."

"I'll bet she's excited about the big one-one," Wren said. "I still remember the day my magic manifested. There's nothing like it. If I could bottle that exhilaration and sell it, I'd be a billionaire."

"She's anxious, to be honest," I said. "She's been looking forward to this day from the first moment she knew it was a possibility. Now that it's so close, I think she might feel overwhelmed by the reality."

"I'd be happy to talk to her, if you like," Wren said. "I've counseled a lot of young witches and wizards through the early stages of magic. It's one of the reasons your aunt chose me to tutor you."

"You're great, Wren, but I doubt that was the main reason," I said.

His brow knitted. "What do you mean?"

"You're a handsome young wizard," I said. "I have an aunt obsessed with marrying Roses off to desirable members of the coven."

He grinned. "Oh, I'm desirable, am I?"

"According to Raoul," I said. "Anyway, I have no doubt this was an attempt at a set-up."

He cocked his head. "Then how do you explain Marigold and Hazel?"

"To make you look even more alluring," I said with a laugh.

"Well, I'm sorry to disappoint your aunt," Wren said. "That's one witch I'd never want to cross."

"Don't worry, Wren," I said. "You're not the disappointment. That's definitely me." And Marley, too, if she failed to come into her magic. I couldn't bear the thought. It was one thing for me to bear the brunt of Aunt Hyacinth's displeasure, but I didn't want Marley subjected to it as well.

Wren gazed at the lighthouse in the distance. "To be perfectly honest, Ember, I wouldn't want to date anyone in your family, no matter how adorable and charming." He gave me a pointed look. "There's too much expectation and ceremony over at Thornhold. It wouldn't suit me." He tucked his wand away. "If you ask me, the sheriff is perfect for you. He can handle your aunt and you with one squint of his eye."

I bristled. "No one *handles* me, thank you very much. I'm not a circus animal."

"That's not how I meant it." He peered past me. "Oh, your friend's back."

Raoul looked down at his body. *Can you see me now? I got tired of waving.*

"I can see you."

Good. I'm ready for you to make good on my pizza now.

On one condition, I said.

Raul gave me a suspicious look. *What's that?*

"That you let me glamour you again when you eat the pizza," I said. "I want to see Marley's face when she catches a turtle eating pizza at the table."

Raoul laughed. *I'm totally in.*

CHAPTER SIX

"REMIND me again why you need me to accompany you, miss?" Simon sat beside me in the passenger seat as I drove us to the Rollins-Mahoney estate.

"Because you speak butlerese," I said. "I'm going to interview Sampson under the guise of finishing my article on his former employer for the paper, but I'm really trying to figure out if he killed her."

"Oh, my. I see."

"The sheriff told me that Sampson was spotted at Charmed, I'm Sure last week," I said. "The clerk said he bought a few items, so I'd like to see if I can get more details."

"What would the butler have to gain from killing his mistress?" Simon asked.

I shrugged. "Who knows? Maybe he was tired of being bossed around."

"That's an essential part of the job, Miss Ember."

"You're a professional," I said. "Maybe Sampson got fed up. He certainly had access and opportunity, living in the house. He also cleaned everything up quickly after her death."

Simon stiffened, appearing to take my suggestion as a personal affront to butlers everywhere. "He was merely doing his job. I doubt he stopped to consider the implications."

I gave him a pointed look. "Or he was destroying evidence and making it look as though he was just doing his job. Use your Jedi power and see if you can sense anything."

"My what, miss?"

I blew a raspberry. "Forget it."

Simon gazed out the window. "It feels strange to sit on this side of a car. A different view all together."

"I guess it is." I fixed him with a hard stare. "You're not going to tell Aunt Hyacinth that I've butler-knapped you, are you? You and I both know she'll have an opinion."

"I informed her that I had an appointment with the healer, miss," Simon said.

My jaw dropped. "You lied for me? Simon, whatever next?"

"A white lie, miss," Simon said. "No harm shall come of it."

"It shouldn't hurt her feelings for you to accompany her niece on an important mission," I said. "After all, the article is for *her* paper."

"I understand, miss," he said, "but you know how your aunt can be."

Oh, I did. No explanation required. "Well, I appreciate you sticking your neck out for me."

"You've done that much and more for me, miss. I'm only happy to return the favor."

I parked in the long driveway and Simon and I walked up to the front door. He instinctively moved to open the door for me but caught himself in time. Instead, he rang the door-bell. A moment later, Sampson opened the door. He still wore his uniform. Part of me expected him to appear in a jogging suit and an earring, or something completely un-butlerlike.

"Good day, miss." He bowed slightly.

"Hey there, Sampson," I said. "This is my friend, Simon. We were hoping to interview you for the article I'm writing about Hattie."

He frowned. "You don't have sufficient material already?"

"Now that she's dead, I figure those around her might be more willing to speak up," I said. "She was such an imposing figure during her lifetime."

Sampson strangled a laugh. "Indeed. Please come in."

We stepped inside the foyer and I noticed that the chandelier was back in its original place and full of sparkle. I pointed upward.

"Who had the chandelier fixed?" I asked.

"I did, miss," Sampson said. "I'm still responsible for keeping the house in order, whether there's a gap in ownership or not."

I glanced at Simon, who gave me a quick nod to confirm. We followed him into the formal living room. Everything appeared exactly as it had when I'd been here for the party. Not a tasteful knickknack out of place.

"You're doing an excellent job of maintaining this place," I said.

"To be fair, miss, I have far fewer tasks now that my mistress is no longer with us. It's no trouble to complete my daily tasks and have time left for myself."

"Do you happen to know which family member inherits the house?"

"Ella, miss. Her great-niece."

That came as a surprise. "Do you plan to stay on after Ella moves in?" I asked.

"Absolutely," he said, his round head bobbing up and down. "I look forward to serving the young miss. She'll be a breath of fresh air." He clamped his mouth shut, realizing how it sounded. "I only mean that I haven't served a young paranormal in quite a long time."

"I understand," Simon said, and I wondered how old Aunt Hyacinth was when she took control of Thornhold.

"Forgive my manners," Sampson said. "I admit to being slightly off kilter ever since…" He faltered. "Can I offer you any refreshments?"

"None for me, thanks," I said. "If you don't mind, I'd like to take a peek at the mead cellar. Maybe snap a few pictures for the article."

Sampson blinked. "The mead cellar? Why, miss?"

"Because it's such an interesting aspect of the story," I said. "A private cellar of fizzlewick mead that no one was allowed to touch except the owner? And that seems to be what was used to kill her."

Sampson looked uneasy. "My mistress always had a strange obsession with keeping the mead to herself. I never understood it myself. Then again, it wasn't my job to understand. Only attend."

"You have one of the keys, right?" I asked.

Sampson nodded and fished a small set from his right jacket pocket. "These are the special keys. My mistress had one to the cellar as well, though she never used it. She wore it on a chain around her neck."

"Interesting choice of jewelry," Simon murmured.

That corresponded to what Fitz had told me. "And how often were you sent to the mead cellar?" I asked, as we followed him to a staircase. We started down the narrow, winding steps.

"Once a year, miss. Always the morning of her birthday."

So if Sampson didn't do it, whoever snuck in must have stolen the key and returned it before then, knowing that Sampson would go down there the morning of her birthday. "What time did you go down the morning of the party?"

"Approximately nine-thirty," he said.

"And what time did Avonne join Hattie for breakfast?" I asked.

"Eight-thirty," Sampson said. "I made sure to have breakfast prepared for them in advance because I had other duties that morning with the party."

We arrived at the base of the staircase and Sampson unlocked an old, wooden door to the right. It creaked open and he turned on a single light bulb overhead. A few cobwebs caught my attention.

"I guess she didn't like you to clean in here," I said.

"No, she preferred to keep the door locked," Sampson said. "It wasn't my place to question household decisions, not when they were made by my employer."

"What about Fitzgerald?" I asked. "His man cave is down here. You don't think he found a way into the stock at any point?" I didn't mention the equipment I discovered in his place.

Sampson laughed. "Oh, he tried in his younger years, but he was easily thwarted. Master Fitz is not as a clever as he likes to believe."

"You don't think he'd be capable of pilfering a key and tampering with the mead?" I asked.

"Not likely, miss. If no other reason than he's far too lazy." There didn't seem to be any love lost between those two.

"Where do you keep the key when you're not in uniform?" Simon asked. A-ha! A butler question.

"In the top drawer of my nightstand," Sampson said.

"Is it routinely locked?" Simon asked.

"No, but then again, I'm the only one in my room. My quarters are quite private and I only spend time in there at the end of the day, after all my work is finished. The rest of the time, I carry the keys with me."

"Where's your room located? I guess it's not downstairs like in all those English movies," I said.

Simon and Sampson both blinked at me.

"My room is at the southeast end of the house, miss," Sampson said.

"It seems like Hattie wasn't exactly beloved by her family," I said. Not that I planned to say as much in the article. It seemed especially cruel now that she'd been murdered.

"My mistress had conflicts with everyone in the family," Sampson admitted. "She seemed to thrive on the fear and power." His expression soured. "I suppose I can say that now, although I still feel a sense of loyalty toward her. My true obligation, however, is to the house."

"Too right," Simon said.

"How about you?" I asked. "Did you have issues with Hattie?"

Sampson hesitated. "Aside from years of thankless servitude, you mean?"

"Did she leave anything to you in her will?" I asked. "Maybe not so thankless after all?"

"I wouldn't know, miss," Sampson replied. "The reading hasn't taken place yet."

"Has anyone seen the will yet?" I asked.

"Not yet, miss," the butler replied. "I only know about Miss Ella from other conversations."

"Who has a copy of the will?" I asked.

"The family's lawyer, Margery Robson. She's on Wisteria Lane."

Now for the big question. "I understand you were seen in Charmed, I'm Sure the week before the murder," I said.

"I was," Sampson replied smoothly, "and the sheriff is now

in receipt of my purchases. No accelerant potions among them."

Oh. I hadn't caught up with the sheriff on recent developments. I should probably compare notes.

"Why did you clean up so quickly after Hattie's death?" I asked. "You whisked away the glass she drank from like you had something to hide." Okay, maybe the question was a little leading, but I wasn't law enforcement.

"Habit, miss," Sampson said. "I always attended to my mistress first. I was also in shock." He wrung his hands. "I believe I still am."

"You said everyone had conflicts with Hattie," I reminded him. "Were there any more recent issues that you can recall? Any particularly nasty squabbles?"

Sampson pursed his lips. "There was a rather heated argument with Master Stone about two weeks before the party."

My antennae lifted. "Avonne's husband?"

"Yes, I don't know the details, unfortunately. I was in the parlor room at the time and they were in the adjoining room —Hattie's office. The raised voices got my attention. Hattie was demanding that he come clean, or something of that nature."

"About what?" I asked.

Sampson's gaze dropped to the floor. "That I don't know. She and Master Stone often discussed his business because it was a safe topic."

I frowned. "Safe in what way?"

"Unlikely to end in an argument," Sampson said. "So many of my mistress's discussions ended up in arguments and Stone is an imposing figure. I think he intimidated her, though she'd never have admitted it. She was too proud."

"So she wanted to stay on his good side?"

"Typically, yes," Sampson said. "I know she made a particular effort. She bought him special shirts with the family colors. Praised his keen business sense. Tried to appeal to his self-made pride."

"Except the day they argued, apparently," I said. "What is Stone's business?"

"He owns Divine Beverage Distributors," Sampson replied. "It's a regional company, I believe, which is why Master Stone travels often for work. Very successful."

"Like Sterling," I murmured to Simon.

"My mistress was visibly shaken when Master Stone left that day," Sampson said, "but I would never have asked about it. That's not my role."

"Quite right," Simon said.

I glanced at Simon. "If Aunt Hyacinth were obviously upset about something, you wouldn't talk to her about it?"

"No, miss," Simon said firmly. "I would bring her a fizzlewick martini."

I rolled my eyes. "Naturally."

"My role was to pretend I saw nothing," Sampson said. "I couldn't even acknowledge it with a cocktail or my mistress would lose her temper."

"She sounds seriously unpleasant," I said. "Why do the horrible ones live to be two hundred?"

"And who knows how much longer she would have carried on if not for this murderous interference?" Sampson remarked.

"How fortunate for you," I said.

"No, miss," Sampson replied. "How fortunate for everyone."

Dinner at Thornhold took on extra meaning for me in light of Hattie's birthday party. I looked around the table at my family and wondered whether they harbored the same ill will toward Aunt Hyacinth that the Rollins-Mahoney clan seemed to feel toward Hattie. I didn't think so, and, yet, there were striking similarities. Tonight, the role of Ember Rose at Hattie's party was being played by none other than Alec Hale. My aunt had invited Alec and Holly, but, interestingly, Alec had darkened Thornhold's doorstep without her.

"I appreciate everyone coming midweek to dine together," Aunt Hyacinth said, standing at the head of the table. "In light of Marley's special day this weekend, I thought it best to preserve Sunday for her first taste of magic. I expect to see her riding her unicorn around the estate and brandishing her first wand like a proper witch."

Marley's broad smile said it all. The eager anticipation rolled off her in waves.

"I guess I've been doing it all wrong then," I murmured. "I don't have a unicorn."

"Plenty of others wouldn't object to being ridden by you," Florian whispered. "Including the vampire across the table."

I kicked my cousin's shin without looking at him and heard a high-pitched yelp beside me. "He has vampire hearing, you nitwit," I hissed. I'd already taken great pains to shield my thoughts from him. He didn't need to know how delicious he looked in his finely tailored blue suit. Well, let's face it—he already knew. I just wasn't going to confirm it.

"This evening, I'd like us all to go around the table and name something we're grateful for," my aunt said.

I balked. "Is this Starry Hollow Thanksgiving or something?"

"What's Thanksgiving?" Hudson asked.

"An American holiday in the human world," Marley said. "It started as a harvest festival, when the Native Americans feasted with the Pilgrims—the English settlers. It was a day of giving thanks for their many blessings."

"Better than being feasted on," Hudson said with a laugh.

"That sounds lovely, Marley," Aunt Hyacinth said. "I think we could all do with a bit of counting our blessings, which is why I decided to entertain the idea at dinner."

Hattie's death must've really struck a chord with my aunt. This was so unlike her.

"I'll start," Florian said. "I'm grateful for this sumptuous meal we're about to enjoy, for the expensive wine to wash it down with, and for the beautiful fairy I'm going to see afterward."

I rolled my eyes. "Another fairy? Is this what happens in the wake of your breakup with Delphine?"

"Nothing wrong with fairies," Florian said. "You have no idea how flexible those wings can be. Inspiring stuff." Was he as bad as Fitz? No, certainly not.

"What about you, Ember?" my aunt asked, eager to move on from her son.

"I'm grateful for the obvious things—my fabulous daughter. A roof over my head. Loved ones around me." I smiled across the table at Alec. "A boss I don't despise."

"My beautiful family," Sterling said. "The fantastic two-week trip Aster and I were able to take and reconnect." He leaned over and kissed her shoulder.

"Same for me," Aster said, beaming at him. They seemed much happier now that they'd taken active steps to work on their marriage.

"I'm grateful for pea soup," Ackley said. "Because I can use it to look like vomit."

"That's gross," Aspen said.

"You're gross," his brother shot back. They began elbowing each other fiercely.

"That's enough, boys," Aster said in a sharp tone. The twins immediately went still.

"I'm grateful for the chance to meet a witch like Linnea," Rick said. The minotaur gazed lovingly at her. "If anyone had told me I had a chance with her, I wouldn't have believed it. She's out of my league, as far as I'm concerned."

I glanced quickly at my aunt, wondering whether she'd make some acerbic remark. To her credit, she remained silent.

"I'm grateful for my sensible, well-behaved children," Linnea said. "It could easily have gone the other way, given their genetics." She laughed. "I'm teasing, kids. And I'm grateful to be a member of this family and for finding someone like Rick, who not only loves me unconditionally, but proves it every day." She slid her hand over top of his.

"Relationship goals," Florian breathed.

"Liar," I said. "If those were your goals, you would've settled down with Delphine."

"I said goals, not imminent deadlines," Florian replied.

"I'm grateful for doing well in school and my family and friends," Bryn said. "And for the car that I'll be getting for my next birthday." She batted her eyelashes at her mother.

"Nice try," Linnea replied.

"I'm grateful for sports," Hudson said. "The end."

Alec's gaze swept the table. "I am eternally grateful for a long, well-lived life and the opportunity to indulge my fantasies and earn a rather nice living from them."

"I'm grateful for those, too," Marley said.

"What a coincidence?" Florian said. "I'm grateful for the chance to indulge my fantasies, too." I punched my cousin in the thigh and he winced. "You're going to be the death of me, Ember."

"I'm grateful for this family," Marley said. "I don't know how our lives would have turned out in New Jersey." Her eyes met mine. "I mean, I know my mom would've done a great job with me no matter what, but Starry Hollow is so much better." She smiled like a lunatic and, in that moment, I recognized myself in her. The apple didn't fall far from the crazy tree. "Plus magic! I'm soooo grateful for magic."

"Be grateful once you have it," I said carefully.

"And why wouldn't she have it?" my aunt asked. "She's a Rose, after all."

I cringed. She wasn't just a Rose. She had a father named Karl. A human father.

"What about you, Aunt Hyacinth?" Marley asked. "What are you grateful for?"

My aunt placed her fingertips lightly on the end of the table. "Thank you for asking, my dear. I am grateful for our proud heritage, for my position in this community, and for my loving family. I have not always handled family disagreements in the best way—Ember's life is proof of that—but I am thankful for the opportunity to set things right. I miss my brother. I miss my husband. But I have all of you and my beloved familiar, and I don't take any of it for granted, though it sometimes might seem that way."

I sat there, stunned. I'd never heard so much honesty and emotion from my aunt in one short speech. And she rarely mentioned my father.

"Thank you, Mother," Linnea said. "We're very touched."

My aunt raised her cocktail glass. "As Alec said, to a life well-lived, and the warm embrace of love all around us."

We raised our glasses and toasted. I couldn't see Hattie's family in quite the same light as this. There'd been something missing from that birthday gathering. A feeling—a connection. Whatever it was, I felt it here tonight and I was grateful for that, too. My aunt probably had less reason to worry than she believed.

The conversation during dinner flowed as quickly and easily as the booze, and I was reminded of how engaging my family could be. Even the children were on their best behavior. The twins managed not to spill anything and Hudson and Bryn refrained from arguing. Much. It was a wonderful evening.

"As lovely as this dinner has been, I'm afraid I must take my leave," Alec said. "I have edits to push through tonight and any more wine will be the death knell for my brain power."

"Understood," Aunt Hyacinth said. "Thank you for your company. You know how much I value you as an employee, but also as a friend."

Alec inclined his head.

"I'll walk you out," I said. "I want to update you on my article."

"Oh, you want to update him, do you?" Florian whispered. "'Update' is a euphemism I haven't used yet."

I gave him a threatening look before leaving the table and joining Alec in the foyer. "I now understand why you chose me to write the article on Hattie," I said.

Alec offered a half smile. "I told you that all would become clear. Have I ever lied to you, Miss Rose?"

"No, never." Inwardly, I sighed. "Honest to a fault." We stepped outside and stood under a canopy of stars. They didn't call this town Starry Hollow for nothing.

"I knew you were the right choice for the article because of your experience here," Alec said. "Of course, I had no idea that the social event would turn into such a prime assignment. Bentley is undoubtedly kicking himself."

I laughed. "I enjoy that part the most."

His mouth twitched. "I imagine so."

"Why no Holly this evening?" I hated to ask...Bah! Who was I kidding? I didn't hate to ask. I was nosy, especially after their office fight.

"Holly has been...under the weather recently," he said. "I thought it best to come alone, although I did appreciate that your aunt extended an invitation to her. I don't take it lightly."

"Gods forbid," I said.

The vampire gazed at me with his usual intensity and I felt my insides warm. "You look very pretty this evening, Miss Rose," he said and then immediately closed his eyes in frustration. "My apologies. I shouldn't have said that."

"You're allowed to pay compliments," I said. "You look as handsome as ever. That's just a fact."

His sensual lips eased into a smile. "I would much rather you be less attractive to me. It would make both of our lives easier."

"And I would much rather you look like a sloth with a hangover, but we don't all get what we want." I shrugged. "That's life."

He stood there watching me for a moment, bathed in moonlight. He appeared ethereal in the golden glow, more like an angel than a demon. "Goodnight, Miss Rose," he finally said.

My heart pounded. "Goodnight, Alec."

CHAPTER SEVEN

MARGERY ROBSON'S office was an attractive building on the corner of Wisteria Lane and Black Cauldron Road. It looked more like a residence than a law office with its white shutters and wraparound front porch. I was tempted to take a turn on the porch swing.

"Let's try to maintain a professional decorum," the sheriff said, as though reading my mind.

"I don't know," I said, gazing at the porch swing. "We are courting, after all. A porch swing seems like a necessity."

He crooked a finger at me. "Come on, Rose. We're trying to investigate a murder, remember?"

"Maybe I should've come with Bolan," I grumbled. "He would've taken a turn on the swing." I laughed to myself. "I can just imagine his tiny little legs not even skimming the porch."

The sheriff tapped his foot. "You finished, Rose?"

I cleared my throat. "Sorry. Professional decorum has been initiated." I smoothed the front of my clothes and headed inside.

The secretary was a gnome by the name of Albert with

thinning hair and thick glasses. "Is Ms. Robson expecting you?" he asked.

The sheriff pointed to the star affixed to his chest. "I'm not in her calendar, but I guarantee you she'll want to speak to me about Hattie Rollins-Mahoney."

Albert pushed out his fat lower lip. "Such a shame. Made it all the way to two hundred and then didn't get to enjoy a slice of cake."

"Did you have a lot of interaction with Hattie?" I asked.

"Here and there over the years," Albert said. "Mostly, Ms. Robson went to see her at the estate. Hattie preferred everyone come to her."

"Was that an age-related thing?" I asked.

Albert chuckled. "No, miss. I'm fairly certain that was a privilege-related thing." He pressed a button on the desk. "Ms. Robson, I have Sheriff Nash and his associate here to see you."

"Thank you, Albert. Please send them in," came the quick reply.

Albert directed us to the office at the end of the corridor. "No need to knock," the gnome said. "Just go right in."

"Thank you," the sheriff said. We walked past a few other offices and several impersonal paintings of flowers. Snooze art.

"Sheriff Nash, so good to see you." Margery Robson crossed the room to shake his hand with both of hers. The slender werefox was average height and her auburn hair had a streak of white running through it. She shifted her focus to me. "Well now, you're not Deputy Bolan. I'd recognize that little green man anywhere."

I stifled a laugh. "I'm Ember Rose, a reporter for *Vox Populi*."

She pointed a finger at me. "Yes, you're the long-lost Rose. I've heard about you."

"All good things, I'd imagine," the sheriff said.

"Depends on your definition of good, I suppose," Margery said, returning to the chair behind her desk.

The alarm in my head sounded. "Excuse me?"

"I'm kidding," Margery said, laughing. "There's no such thing as a bad Rose, in my experience."

"Do you know my family?" I asked.

"Not as well as I'd like," the werefox replied. "I've tried to court your legal business over the years, but I haven't been able to make inroads."

"Once someone has earned my aunt's loyalty, it's difficult to sway her," I said. As challenging as Aunt Hyacinth could be, that was still one of her best qualities, as far as I was concerned. She'd think nothing of throwing her weight around for a friend or trusted employee.

"Have a seat," Margery said. She motioned to the two plush chairs in front of the desk. "I don't suppose you're here for a prenuptial agreement."

The sheriff coughed. "No, no. Nothing like that."

Margery glanced from the sheriff to me. "You are an item, though, aren't you? I can smell the chemistry from here."

Sheriff Nash tried to relax, but he was clearly thrown off track. "Why don't we focus on the reason for our visit? I need to see the will of Hattie Rollins-Mahoney."

Margery seemed blasé about the request. "I was wondering when you'd get around to paying me a visit. I was beginning to think the rumors weren't true."

"Which rumors are those?" the sheriff asked.

"That Hattie didn't die of natural causes," the lawyer said. "She was murdered. I've delayed the reading and the accountant has frozen all of Hattie's assets."

"Sounds like you have experience with this sort of thing," the sheriff said.

"Before your time, Sheriff," Margery said. "Any leads? I mean, the woman was two hundred. What was the point?"

The sheriff wore a sympathetic expression. "Maybe someone tired of waiting for the reading of the will."

Margery lifted a thick document off the desk. "I have it right here. I was reviewing it earlier today, in fact. There's nothing earth shattering in it that I can see. Most of the contents are known to the family already."

The sheriff held out his hand. "May I?"

Margery hesitated. "There's no point in making you jump through hoops for this, is there?"

"Wouldn't help anybody," the sheriff said.

Margery nodded and handed over the document. "I don't know if this'll really help you anyway. Like I said, nothing is a surprise."

Sheriff Nash flipped through the will. "Just the grandkids named in here or others, too?"

"Ella, her great-niece, and Sampson, her butler are included." Margery looked thoughtful. "Sampson only takes a small share, though."

"Nothing specific to the great-grandchildren?" I asked.

"No." Margery clasped her hands on her desk. "She wasn't overly fond of children. Sometimes I wonder whether she'd have excluded the grandchildren had they still been minors upon her death."

"Any conditions on the distribution?" the sheriff asked.

"A couple that have already been satisfied," Margery said. "If Lacey was still married to Weston, she would've been disinherited. If Fitzgerald had married a non-nymph, he would have been excluded. Those conditions won't extend beyond the distribution, though. Once Fitzgerald gets his share, he can marry a Kraken if he wants."

"I can't believe Hattie cared that much," I said. "It seems ridiculous."

"She liked to exercise control over her family," Margery explained. "After her daughter and son-in-law died in that tragic accident, Hattie grew more rigid in her approach to the family. Their deaths weighed on her, I think, and she wanted to make sure that no one made any grave mistakes."

"Mistakes like marrying a shifter instead of a nymph?" I queried. "That hardly seems on par with guilt over a yachting accident."

Margery nodded. "I agree with you, but Hattie was my client with a mind of her own. As long as it didn't contravene the law, I followed her wishes."

"You never tried to talk her out of anything?" the sheriff asked.

"Are you kidding?" Margery looked appalled by the suggestion. "Hattie would've fired me without a second thought. She was accustomed to getting her way in every aspect of life. Another reason I think she took her daughter's death so hard. It was a blow to her ego on top of the normal cycle of grief and loss."

I couldn't imagine feeling so privileged that I thought I was above loss and tragedy. Death came for us all eventually, and rarely in the order we expected.

"Mind if I take a copy of this?" the sheriff asked.

"Feel free. I have extras for the family," Margery said. "Is there any reason to delay the reading longer?"

"Go ahead with the reading," the sheriff said, "but the distribution itself will have to wait until the murder has been solved. Obviously, the guilty party can't inherit."

"Assuming the murderer is named in the will," Margery said.

The sheriff gave her a half smile. "I think the odds are pretty good, don't you?"

. . .

After our visit with Margery, the sheriff and I parted ways. He had to handle a brawl at the Whitethorn that got out of hand, so I decided to drive over to Divine Beverage Distributors to question Stone Beauregard. His office was located on the fringe of Starry Hollow in a building that seemed like more of a warehouse than a business. The receptionist behind the front desk was a gruff-looking troll by the name of Gregor.

"Hi, there," I said, adopting my friendliest tone. "I'm hoping to squeeze in five minutes with Stone Beauregard. Is he around, by any chance?"

"You got an appointment?" Gregor asked. His voice was so deep, I was pretty sure it reverberated inside me.

"No, I was in the neighborhood and thought I'd drop in," I said. "I'd like to see how he's doing after his grandmother-in-law's death. Is that a word? Grandmother-in-law?"

A fairy fluttered past behind the reception desk and seemed to stop mid-air. "You're here for Stone?" she asked. I didn't miss the flash of annoyance across her delicate features. She was pretty, with an attractive figure, and wavy, blond hair with purple tips to match her wings.

"Yes, that's right. I'm Ember Rose, a reporter with *Vox Populi*. Stone and I met at Hattie's birthday party."

"It's all right, Gregor," the fairy said. "I'll escort her back."

Gregor grunted a response.

"Thanks," I said. "I didn't mean to drop by unannounced."

"Then maybe you shouldn't have," the fairy said. "Stone is a very busy man. He barely has time to eat his meals, let alone entertain unexpected guests during business hours."

Her tone was so hostile that I knew there had to be a story. "And what do you do here?" I asked casually.

"I'm the Director of Marketing," she said. "Fern Galloway."

"Nice to meet you, Fern." But not really.

She made a disgruntled noise before stopping in front of an office door. She cracked it open and poked her nose in. "Stone? There's a woman here to see you by the name of Ember Rose."

"Thank you so much, Fern," I said. "I really appreciate your help."

Fern gave me a haughty look before allowing me entry. "Do you need me to stay?"

Stone frowned. "For a meeting with a reporter about Hattie? Whatever for, Fern?" He seemed genuinely dismissive of her.

Fern's jaw set. "Fine then. I'm going back to my office." Her wings seemed to flutter a mile a minute, expressing her dismay. She slammed the door behind me for good measure.

I gave Stone a curious look. "She works for you, huh?"

Stone offered a sheepish grin. "Some fairies can be temperamental."

"My office manager is a fairy and she's unfailingly pleasant," I replied.

"Have a seat," he said. "I suspect you're here to talk more about Hattie, now that it's a murder investigation."

"Very astute," I said.

"The sheriff's already been by this week," Stone said. "That deputy has a real chip on his shoulder about being small and green. I can't help it if he's a leprechaun. It's nothing to do with me."

I suppressed a smile. "Like fairies, some leprechauns can be temperamental." I sat in the red leather chair across from him. "I understand you had an argument with Hattie the week of her death."

Stone looped his pen through his fingers. "Where did you hear that? Sampson? That butler is always lurking in the shadows."

"It doesn't matter," I said. "Can you tell me what the argument was about?"

Stone hesitated. "Hattie being Hattie."

"And what does that mean?" I asked.

"The old morgen was trying to control everyone's lives. She had nothing better to do with her time, so she got involved in everyone's business."

"And what was she trying to control this time?" I asked.

He dropped the pen. "She found out about a corporate opportunity that I was considering. A larger company offered to buy us out. Pippin Enterprises. They also requested that I join their corporate headquarters in Starlight City."

"That's not nearby, I guess?"

"No, about twelve hundred miles away," he replied. "Hattie found out and was furious that I'd even consider it. She didn't want Avonne moving away from Starry Hollow."

"Did you talk to Avonne about it?" I asked.

He shook his head. "I didn't want to raise the issue until I knew how I felt about it. If I decided not to do it, I didn't want to bother discussing it."

That made sense. "And what happened?"

"I decided not to go ahead," he replied.

"Because of Hattie?"

"No, but I'll admit that her objection was on my mind." He put his feet up on the desk and rested his hands behind his head. "Avonne and the kids are my priority. If they didn't want to go, I wouldn't have gone anyway."

"How did your employees feel? Did Fern think you'd made a bad business decision?" Maybe that was why she seemed hostile. Resentment toward her employer.

"Fern liked the idea of moving to a new place," he said. When I expressed surprise, he waved his hand. "They offered positions to all senior staff and that included Fern."

"What kinds of beverages do you distribute?" I asked. Judging from the posters on the wall, it included a variety of alcoholic beverages.

"Nectar, mead, a variety of divine beverages," Stone said. "It's a popular market. Everyone assumes ale is the money-maker, but I recognized their untapped potential."

"You do very well, I hear."

He placed his feet back on the ground. "How do you think I managed to land a morgen like Avonne Rollins-Mahoney? Do you think she would've settled for some shifter mechanic?"

"Her sister did," I said. Not that Weston was a mechanic, but he certainly wasn't rich.

"And look what happened to them," Stone said. "Trust me, I saw what happened with Lacey and Weston. I didn't want that to happen to Avonne and me, so I've made it my mission to stay on Hattie's good side."

"In what way?" I asked. I was genuinely curious how anyone stayed on Hattie's good side. Maybe pick up a few tips for Aunt Hyacinth.

"I wore whatever ugly shirt she gave me. You saw the color-mad shirt I had on for her party. I did anything to impress her. I bought her expensive gifts. Brought her mead and nectar from here, in fact. I was willing to go the distance for the sake of my marriage."

"So she really had a good side you could tap into?" I queried.

Stone raked a hand through his hair. "I know she seemed salty, but she could be sweet when the mood struck her."

"Once in a blue moon?" I asked.

He laughed. "Seems like you know the type."

"Did she ever let you taste her special mead, given your business?" I asked.

He lowered his head. "One of my biggest regrets. She

hoarded that fizzlewick mead like a dragon and its treasure." He held up a finger. "One time she let me down in the cellar to see the inventory, but I wasn't allowed to taste it."

"That's too bad," I said. "You're the perfect one to assess it."

"I know, right?" He sighed. "Maybe now I'll finally get a chance, depending on who controls it."

"Does the will mention it specifically?" I asked.

"I don't know," Stone said. "I haven't been privy to the contents. There's been a delay because of the investigation."

"Are you expecting anything?" I asked.

"Don't need anything," he replied. "I have all the money I could want. The perfect wife. The perfect life, really. That's why I ultimately decided not to risk it with Pippin Enterprises. Nothing is worth rocking this yacht."

"I don't blame you," I said. "You seem to have a pretty good thing going here."

He bumped his fist lightly against his chest. "I still think about the moment that chandelier fell. If anything had happened to me, what would've become of Avonne and the children?"

"Well, they have Rollins-Mahoney money," I said.

"True," he replied, "but to live a life without each other." He shuddered. "Of course, I saved Hattie, but for what?" He covered his face with his hands. "The whole thing still feels like a waking nightmare. Avonne's been so distraught. She's worried about her kids. Her start-up costs…."

My head snapped to attention. "Her start-up costs?"

He moved his hands back to the desk. "For her new business venture."

"What is it?" I asked.

"A children's clothing line," Stone replied. "She's always loved fashion and I think she figured if she could make a financial success of it, she wouldn't be as beholden to her grandmother."

"Why not get the funding from you?" I asked. If she didn't want to be beholden to her grandmother, borrowing money from the elderly morgen wasn't the smart play.

"Avonne didn't want me to fund it," he said. "She knows I'm self-made and she didn't want to use me to build her business. And I support her independence. It sets a good example for the children."

"But is it really independence if she was relying on her grandmother for the seed money?" I asked.

He leaned forward and lowered his voice. "I heard you live in a cottage on your aunt's estate and you work for her paper. Is that true?"

Ooh, Stone was smarter than his muscles implied. "Fair enough," I said, bristling. "Though I was sort of dropped into the middle of Starry Hollow unexpectedly. I wasn't born with a silver spoon in my mouth." Or whatever wealthy morgens were born with.

"Neither was I," Stone said. "And it feels good to make my own way in the world, let me tell you. Her grandmother never held real power over me as a result, and it's a welcome feeling."

"I guess she doesn't hold power over anyone anymore," I said.

Stone exhaled through his nostrils. "No. Hattie's reign of terror is finally over."

CHAPTER EIGHT

THAT NIGHT, my dreams were fraught with barrels of mead and nectar. I was running on top of them as they spun on their sides, like I was a cartoon hamster going nowhere fast. There were shadows behind me, but I couldn't stop running long enough to get a good look at them.

I felt a presence in the doorway of my bedroom and bolted upright. "Who's there?" My eyes focused and I realized it was Marley. More importantly, her eyes glistened with tears. "Marley, what's wrong?"

"It's my birthday," she declared. She ran into my room and threw herself lengthwise across my bed.

"Happy birthday, sweetheart," I said, still groggy. I drew my knees to my chest to avoid getting smushed by her rolling body. "Why do you look sad?"

"Because I don't feel any different." She pressed her face into the blanket and I heard her muffled cries.

I reached forward and patted her back. "Listen, you weren't born until the afternoon. That means you're not technically eleven yet."

"Are we in the same time zone as New Jersey?" Marley asked.

"We're still on the east coast, so I think so." At least I didn't think there was a special paranormal time zone.

She hastened a glance at me. "What time in the afternoon?"

"Maybe it's best if I don't tell you," I said. "Otherwise, you'll end up watching the clock all day."

She jumped onto her knees on the bed. "Please, Mom." She threaded her fingers together and pleaded. "I promise I won't fixate on the time."

I flipped back the covers and left the bed. "Yes, you will. You get obsessive."

PP3 ran into the room, barking to go outside. Marley scooped him off the floor.

"If I take him out, will you tell me when I come back in?" she asked.

"Nope." I went into the bathroom and closed the door.

"If I promise to give you all my birthday money, will you tell me?" Marley's voice drifted through the small gap under the door.

I leaned down and said, "Nope." I waited until I heard her leave the room to vacate the bathroom. The truth was that Marley had been born in the early hours of the morning. The realization made my heart sink.

Marley had not come into her magic.

It had been different for me. I hadn't known at Marley's age that I was supposed to have magic. My father had hidden our identities. I'd grown up in New Jersey, never knowing my true heritage. Marley, on the other hand, had been waiting for this moment since our arrival in Starry Hollow and the revelation about our family. I had no idea what to do.

I wrapped a robe around me and padded downstairs just as the front door of the cottage blew open.

"Mom, guess who's here?" Marley skipped into the house, clutching a beautifully wrapped gift under her arm. PP3 trotted in behind her, his leash dragging along the floor.

"I hope it isn't too early." Alec ducked as he entered the cottage. His lips curved into a smile when he noticed me in a robe with my special brand of bed hair. "I can see that I should have waited another half an hour."

I ran my fingers through my hair in a lame attempt to tame the runaways. "We're presentable-ish. Come on in."

"I thought it best to stop by on my way to the office and be the first to wish Miss Marley the happiest of birthdays."

"You're the second," I pointed out.

Alec inclined his head. "Yes, of course." His gaze swept the room, as though looking for someone else. Interesting. Did he worry that the sheriff would be here?

"Can I open it now, Mom?" Marley asked. "Please?"

"Yes, but only because Alec is here," I said.

Marley tore off the paper and gasped when she saw Alec's latest book. "Is it for sale yet?" she asked. "Is this an early copy?"

"It is," he replied, "but there's something even better. Open it."

Marley flipped through the pages until she reached the dedication. Her eyes popped when she saw her name. She looked up at Alec, her blue eyes shining. "You dedicated the book to me?"

He ruffled her dark hair. "My number one fan? Of course, why wouldn't I?"

Marley clutched the book to her chest. "This is the most amazing present ever. Thank you so much."

"I hope you love the book," Alec said. "There's a strong female heroine in there and I think you'll appreciate her."

"Like me?" she asked.

Alec gave me a quick look. "And your mom."

Marley laughed. "Well, duh. Where do you think I get it?" She rushed over to the vampire and threw her arms around him. "I love it, Alec. It's the best gift ever."

He stroked the back of her head and I felt my chest tighten at the sight. For whatever reason, Alec was like the surrogate father that Marley had been missing. Although I knew Marley liked the sheriff, I also knew that she had a special place in her heart for the stoic vampire. And Marley had impeccable judgment when it came to people—and paranormals. If only Alec displayed the same openness with me that he did with my daughter.

But he didn't. Or wouldn't.

"How's Holly?" Marley asked. "She didn't want to come with you?"

"As I said, I'm on my way into the office," Alec said uneasily. I didn't need to be a crackerjack reporter to know there was a story buried in that sentence.

"Your home away from home," I said.

He shifted his attention to me. "How is your progress with the article on the Rollins-Mahoney murder? I imagine your…access to the sheriff is helpful in this matter."

"It's coming along," I said. "The article, not the access. Well, I'd be lying if I said there wasn't access, but…."

Alec held up a hand. "No need to elaborate, Miss Rose. I shall leave you both to your morning ritual."

"I can't wait to read this," Marley said, hugging the book. "It'll have to wait until after my sleepover, though. The other girls probably won't like it if I hide in my room and read while they're here."

I patted her head. "You're learning, my little bookworm."

Alec strode to the door. "I look forward to hearing all about the party. I have no doubt the event will be a complete success."

I was glad one of us believed that. With me in charge and Marley's magic on the line, I wasn't convinced.

"That was really thoughtful of him, don't you think?" Marley followed me into the kitchen where I jumped into action on the breakfast front.

"Yes, it was," I said. "You're lucky that he has such great affection for you. He's not like that with many others."

"It's because of the way he feels about you, Mom," Marley said. She sat at the small kitchen table and opened the book. "He'd never have taken such an interest in me if he didn't have feelings for you."

A lump formed in my throat. "Don't be silly, sweetheart. You're a special little girl and Alec is smart enough to recognize that. It has nothing to do with me."

"He'd make an awesome stepdad," Marley said with a sigh. "It's too bad Holly doesn't have kids."

"Well, it's possible he and Holly will have kids of their own eventually." Hearing the words aloud, even from my own mouth, made my stomach turn. I knew it was irrational, but it served no purpose to deny that I felt that way. At least to myself.

"I'm not so sure," Marley said. "I think they're having issues."

"Issues?" I repeated. I couldn't help but smile at Marley's adult vernacular sometimes.

"Couldn't you tell?" Marley asked. She skimmed a few pages of the book. "You should read this mom. I think his main character's love interest is based on you."

"What makes you say that?" I walked around the counter to peer over shoulder.

"For starters, she matches your physical description," Marley said. "Dark hair, light eyes, expressive face."

"That could be anyone," I said.

"Oh, look." Marley giggled. "She's prone to using inappropriate language. That's definitely you."

"Mother of…." I snatched the book from her hands and continued to read the description of the D'handra, the mysterious woman from another land that enters the protagonist's life.

"See?" Marley said, satisfied. "Totally you."

I handed the book back to her. I didn't have time to get caught up in a fantasy world right now. "I'll read it after you. No spoilers." Knowing Alec, he probably kills her off by the end and has the protagonist marry some milquetoast nymph with big boobs named Lolly.

"What time did you say I'd come into my magic?" Marley asked.

I pulled a face. "Nice try." I needed to hurry or Marley wasn't going to have time to eat before school. "I'm saving my magical breakfast skills for tomorrow morning when your friends are here."

"Don't worry, Mom. I warned my friends not to expect anything fancy. I know your culinary skills are limited, even with magic."

"Gee, thanks," I replied. I went to the pantry and pulled out the present I'd carefully hidden there. Marley was an excellent snoop, so I'd had to find somewhere clever to hide her birthday gift.

Marley held out her hands in a gesture that reminded me of when she was a toddler. Instead of handing over the present, I slipped in for a hug. "I love you, birthday girl."

She planted a wet kiss on my cheek. "I love you, too." She wiggled her fingers against my back. "Now grabby hands want present."

I released her and gave her the gift. I watched her unwrap it, unsure how'd she react to what was inside. She pulled out the beautiful ivory picture frame and examined the photograph of the woman cradling an infant.

"Is that you and baby me?" she asked.

"No, that's one of the few photos of my mother with me before she died," I said. "I thought you'd like to have it." I swallowed hard. I hadn't expected to feel so emotional about it.

Marley traced my mother's outline with her finger. "She's so pretty. No wonder we don't look like Roses. We look like her."

I snaked an arm around her shoulder and pulled her close. "We do." Although my mother didn't have the ethereal beauty of my cousins, she had a beauty that was all her own. "I think we would've liked her a lot, too."

"Did Aunt Hyacinth give you the photo?" Marley asked.

I nodded. "From her secret stash."

Marley kissed the picture frame. "Thank you. I'll treasure it always."

The doorbell rang and PP3 raced for the door. "Another surprise visitor?" I murmured.

Florian entered the kitchen before I had a chance to answer the door. He came bearing gifts, including a pink box with a ribbon from the local patisserie.

"I figured sugary baked goods were in order on this special day," he said. He gave Marley a kiss on the cheek. "Happy birthday, little cousin." He set the box in front of her. "I assumed there'd be no objection from the woman in charge."

"I don't object at all," Marley said, opening the box. A shimmering array of baked goods danced their way out and lined up in a row, awaiting Marley's decision.

"They're enchanted, not alive," Florian explained. "So don't be worried about eating them."

"This is so cool," Marley said. She plucked the twisted purple from the air and bit into it.

"Thanks, Florian," I said. "This was really thoughtful."

Florian gave me a knowing smile. "Why, yes, Ember, there's enough for you."

"Hey! I wasn't trying to swipe any of my daughter's birthday breakfast. What kind of mother do you take me for?" I retrieved three plates from the cabinet and set them on the table.

"Was that Alec Hale I saw leaving here at such an early hour?" Florian asked, clucking his tongue. "Whatever would the sheriff say?"

"He didn't stay overnight," Marley said, "although I'm sure he would if Mom asked. He brought me a present." She tapped the book.

"And he left with a present as well," Florian said. "The image of your mother in her morning state. I'll bet he changes his mind about any future sleepovers now."

"You're obsessed with sleepovers at my house," I said. "The only sleepover that we should be concerned with right now is the one happening tonight with six other girls."

Marley hopped up and down in her seat. "I can't wait. It's going to be the best birthday ever." She polished off another dancing baked good and ran upstairs to brush her teeth.

"Is it going to be the best birthday ever, Mom?" Florian asked, giving me a pointed look.

I bit my lip. "I don't know yet, Florian, but I'll say this much—it's not looking good."

CHAPTER NINE

THE SLEEPOVER GUESTS all arrived within ten minutes of each other. Sleeping bags and pillows were chucked along the wall and presents were promptly discarded on the table. I offered each parent the opportunity to stay for a drink, but they all declined. They seemed eager to get to whatever fun activity they'd planned in the absence of at least one child.

Once the girls were present and accounted for, Marley dragged them upstairs for a tour of the cottage. I sat on the sofa, organizing the gift bags and marveling at the change in our lives from only a year ago. There hadn't been six girls sleeping over in our tiny two-bedroom apartment in New Jersey for her tenth birthday. Marley had still been sleeping with me, in fact. Magic or no magic, she'd come into her own in Starry Hollow and I was so proud of the young woman she was becoming. Marley was everything I'd hoped my child would be—strong, compassionate, kind, and insightful. I hated that she was being denied the one thing she wanted most in the world. It seemed fundamentally unfair, and yet there was nothing I could do about it.

The girls eventually paraded downstairs with Marley in

the lead. She was followed by Jenna, Lucy, Pietra, Katy, Allie, and Meg. Although I didn't know them well, they all seemed like nice girls with good heads on their shoulders. Marley tended to choose well when it came to friends. That would be a definite plus as she moved into her teen years.

"We're going into the woods for a bit," Marley said. "They want to see the pond where Florian was stuck as a frog."

"Oh, it's famous, is it?" I asked.

"We never have cool stuff like that happen in our family," Katy said. "I wish elves were magical."

"It's both a blessing and a curse," I said. "So be careful what you wish for."

"I come into my magic in three weeks," Lucy announced. "My parents are planning a big party." She grabbed Marley's arm and jumped and down. "We'll be initiated into the coven together."

Katy nudged Marley. "I hope you come into your magic while we're in the woods. Won't that be awesome?"

"My mom said afternoon, but I think she meant early evening," I heard Marley say as they left the cottage.

My body tensed. Midnight would be here soon enough. What would happen if Marley's magic didn't come?

PP3 growled and I thought one of the girls had returned to the cottage. I opened the door and was surprised to see Simon holding an umbrella over my aunt's head. I peered up at the early evening sun.

"Are you expecting rain?" I asked, stepping aside to allow them entry.

"No, but the sun is brutal on my fair skin," my aunt said. Her white-blond hair was loose today, skimming her shoulders. She wore an aqua blue kaftan with images of lime green cat heads. My aunt swept into the room with her usual regal air, holding a beautifully decorated box. PP3 stood directly in her path and barked. She gave the dog a withering look, prompting him to fall silent. The Yorkshire terrier jumped onto the sofa and curled in a ball, which was basically what I wanted to do whenever my aunt came to visit.

Simon closed the umbrella and left without a word. Aunt Hyacinth handed me the present. "Where is the birthday girl?"

"In the woods with her friends," I said.

My aunt's nose wrinkled. "The woods? What have they done that they're being punished so soon?"

"No, they wanted to explore," I said. I would've been the same at their age. I just didn't have wide-open spaces to explore where I grew up.

"I've been planning her celebration with Simon," Aunt Hyacinth said. "Perhaps now is a good time to review the details with you."

I hesitated. "I'm not sure we should discuss those plans yet."

Aunt Hyacinth stiffened. "Please tell me she's come into her magic today. Florian said there was no sign of it this morning."

I shook my head. "Still waiting."

My aunt sucked in a breath. "Why didn't you alert me to the problem? I could've arranged a healer to be here for a thorough examination."

"I'm not sure there is a problem," I said. "Her magic was never a guarantee, not with a human father."

My aunt's jaw clenched. "No, this is unacceptable. That child is a Rose and she is to inherit the power of the One True Witch. I feel it in my bones."

"I'm glad you do because I don't have any sense of it."

"That's because you're not in touch with your magic," Aunt Hyacinth said. "The more you focus on your lessons, however, the closer you will get. It's one of the reasons your education is so important."

"I thought it was just so I didn't embarrass you," I said.

My aunt made the closest sound to blowing a raspberry she'd deign to make. "That ship has sailed, my darling. I'd simply like you to demonstrate competence and become the witch you were meant to be. I would think you'd want that for yourself as well."

"I guess I wouldn't mind being better at magic," I admitted. I could certainly see how easier my life would be if I could get a handle on conjuring spells.

"You have the ability, Ember," my aunt said. "You only need the focus. Unfortunately, you have far too many distractions in your life."

"Maybe that's Marley's problem," I said. "Too many distractions."

"The child doesn't suffer from your variety," my aunt said pointedly.

I folded my arms. "Are you talking about the sheriff?"

"Granger is one of many," she replied.

I thought of Hattie and her heavy-handed approach to her family. "Would you ever try to force me to marry a wizard? Like threaten to cut Marley out of your will or something?" Because the surest way to coerce me into anything was to use my child as a pawn. I'd cave in a heartbeat.

Aunt Hyacinth appeared taken aback by my forthright question. "As I recall, my dear, you made it quite clear to me that you would do as you please with your personal life, regardless of my opinion."

"I remember," I said. We'd been in her office and I still remembered the surge of adrenalin that had shot through me when I'd dared to speak up. My aunt may be a formidable witch in Starry Hollow, but I was from New Jersey.

"You and Alec seem to have developed a solid friendship, so I know your preferences can't be as banal as they seem."

My thoughts turned to Lacey and Weston. "If I ever chose someone you disapproved of, would you retaliate by holding my actions against Marley?"

My aunt scrutinized me. "What of you? Aren't you concerned that I would choose to exclude *you* from the family fortune?"

I shrugged. "I came from nothing, Aunt Hyacinth. I'm very comfortable with nothing. I just don't want any disagreement that we have to spill over into your relationship with Marley. She's the priority."

My aunt considered me for a moment. "I know it may not seem like it to you, especially given the extreme measures your father took to keep you from here, but I'm not a vindictive witch, Ember. Marley is a member of this family, and the Roses take care of their own."

I relaxed slightly. "I'm glad to hear it. If Hattie's murder has shown me anything, it's that excessive control breeds resentment."

"Hattie has been on my mind as well."

"Yes, I got that impression from dinner the other night," I said.

Aunt Hyacinth cracked a smile. "She was quite the cantankerous old morgen, wasn't she?"

"So much worse than you, if it's any consolation."

My aunt's expression softened. "You and I are still getting acquainted, niece. Relationships such as ours take time and I realize that I'm not an easy woman to get to know. Walls are often quick to go up but slow to come down."

Well, that was an unexpected glimpse of my aunt's self-awareness.

"Speaking of relationships, have you considered wading back into the dating pool?" I asked.

She literally clutched her pearls. "I beg your pardon?"

"Plenty of time has passed since your husband died," I said. "Don't you think it's time to consider new prospects?"

Aunt Hyacinth's laugh was throaty and deep. "My darling niece, my life is sufficiently full without a partner. I couldn't begin to imagine including someone new with my busy schedule. Men like to be pampered and I am not one who pampers."

"What if you met someone who pampered you?"

"That's what I have Simon for," she replied. "And I owe him nothing but a paycheck in return. It's divine." She clicked her fingernails on the top of the chair. "Be sure to give my gift to Marley as soon as she returns. Perhaps it will trigger the Rose genes to take action."

"Thank you, Aunt Hyacinth."

In a rare moment of affection, she walked over and stroked PP3's head. I was fairly certain the dog cringed, but, to his credit, he stayed quiet.

"I hope the party is a wonderful success," my aunt said. "Should you have any trouble, though, Simon and Mrs. Babcock are on call to assist you tonight." She breezed out the door to where Simon awaited her with the fancy version of a rickshaw. If there was a name for that contraption, I had no idea what it was.

I took the opportunity to shake the box while Marley was still in the woods. It had to be something magic-related. My aunt was as obsessed with Marley's potential magic as my daughter was.

"Aren't you a little old to be peeking at presents?" The sheriff's voice startled me and I dropped the box back onto the table. "Sorry, didn't mean to scare you. Your aunt didn't quite close the door." He chuckled. "She probably expected Simon to do it."

PP3 raised his head and let loose a fierce bark. "Calm down," I yelled. "It's just Granger. You know him."

The sheriff swaggered into the cottage and fixed PP3 with a hard look. "Not another word out of you, friend. You and I need to come to a truce if I'm going to be spending more time here."

PP3 seemed to understand, lowering his head back to the sofa cushion.

"The girls are in the woods," I said. "Hopefully not wreaking too much havoc on Mother Nature."

He looped an arm around my waist and drew me close. "How much time do you think we have?"

I gave him a quick kiss on the lips. "Enough for you maybe, but not enough for me."

He grinned. "You're probably right about that."

"Way to keep a lady interested."

He produced a small package from his back pocket. "This is my birthday offering." He set it on the table beside the box from my aunt.

"That's sweet, Granger," I said. "You shouldn't have felt obligated to bring her anything, though."

"Hey, I remember being eleven," he replied. "I would've held a grudge for years if the guy in love with my mom didn't bother to get me a birthday present."

We both froze at the same time, realizing the enormity of his admission.

"How about a drink?" I blurted. Sweet baby Elvis. Make mine a double.

The sheriff ignored my question. "Oh, hell, Rose," he said. "I should've saved that declaration for a special occasion."

"Technically, Marley's birthday is a special occasion."

"Not the kind I meant." He seemed mildly flustered, which was both out of character and highly enjoyable to witness.

I didn't know how to respond. It was so unexpected and I

wasn't ready to talk about *feelings*—mostly because that would require being able to identify them.

"I need to get out the paper plates," I said, breaking toward the kitchen. "The food should be here soon."

"What kind of food?" He followed me into the kitchen.

"Pizza," I replied. "I decided to keep some traditions from the human world. Marley should grow up steeped in both cultures."

"I think you're using the term 'culture' a little loosely there, Rose."

I gave his arm a playful smack. "Pizza is a time-honored tradition for birthday parties."

"As long as none of these sprites have any allergies, I'm sure it's a good choice."

I snapped to attention. "Food allergies? How would I know?"

"I guess if nobody mentioned anything, then you're good." He bustled around the kitchen as though he lived here, pulling a jug of punch from the fridge and paper cups from the pantry.

I heard the shouts before the door burst open. Marley hunched over, panting. "We need ointment."

"For what?" I ran over to inspect her.

"Not for me." She struggled to catch her breath. "Pietra is breaking out in hives."

"Why?" I craned my neck. "Where is she?"

"The rest are coming," Marley said. "Katy and I ran ahead to tell you."

I was terrible with emergency kits. I wasn't even sure I had a box of Band-Aids, or whatever the paranormal equivalent was.

More yelling signaled the arrival of Pietra. We moved into the living area where the vampire was sprawled across the sofa. Her legs were covered in red splotches. PP3 quickly relocated without being told.

The sheriff crouched beside her. "Which part of the woods were you in? Did you recognize any of the plants or trees?"

Pietra shook her head. "I'm not usually allowed to play in the woods."

Oops. "Why not?" I asked.

"Because I have severe environmental allergies," Pietra said. "Our house is pretty sterile."

"But you go to school," I said. How could Marley not have mentioned this to me? She was supposed to be the sensible one.

"I have special dispensation to have athletic classes indoors," Pietra said.

"A vampire with environmental allergies," the sheriff said. "Not something I see every day."

"Should I call the healer, Mom?" Marley asked.

The sheriff glanced up at her. "No need, birthday girl. I can handle this one." He faced me. "You got any ironweed and fairy bark?"

"No, but Mrs. Babcock will," I said.

"I'll go," Allie said. The werewolf was likely the fastest of the girls and she knew it. "Do I ring the bell at the main house?"

"Yes, Simon will answer," I said. "Tell him I sent you and what you need."

Allie took off like a shot.

"She's on the track team," Meg said, as though that explained everything.

Pietra began to shift uncomfortably. "I think it's spreading." She lifted her shirt slightly and I could see the red marks growing on her midriff.

"How allergic are you?" I asked. Unattractive skin I could handle. Anaphylactic shock was another matter.

"I don't know which plant is responsible," Pietra said. "I was too focused on the unicorn."

"The unicorn?" I whirled around to eye Marley. "I thought you were going to the woods."

"We did," Marley said, "and we stopped first to get Firefly."

"Where's Firefly now?" I asked.

"Jenna's bringing her back to the stable," Marley said. "She rides regularly so she has lots of experience."

I hadn't even realized Jenna was missing. Some watchful parent I was. "Is anyone allergic to pizza or cake?" I asked. "Please speak now." Thankfully, no one answered.

The doorbell rang and PP3 bolted for the door. I opened the door for the pizza delivery guy just as Allie rushed in with the ingredients from Mrs. Babcock.

"She gave me a few extras, too," Allie said. "That brownie knows her stuff."

I paid for the pizzas and hurried to drop them on the kitchen counter before returning to check on Pietra. My heart was racing from all the activity. What if something happened to Pietra while she was under my care?

By the time I returned to the sofa, I could see that the sheriff had everything under control. He'd already mixed the ingredients and was applying them to Pietra's skin. Some of the splotches on her legs had already faded.

"I feel better," Pietra said. "Thank you, Sheriff Nash."

"Don't mention it," he said. "Emergency aid is all part of the job when you're the sheriff."

Stars and stones. The werewolf was more maternal than I was. He soothed the angry allergic reaction and kept Pietra at ease in the process. Meanwhile, I was still trying to calm my nerves and deal with the fact that the pizza was here—pizza that I didn't even cook myself.

Once Jenna reappeared and Pietra was fully recovered, I brought out the food and drinks and everyone helped themselves. The girls chatted happily while the sheriff and I sequestered ourselves in the kitchen. He took two ales from the pantry and handed one to me.

"You're allowed one on sleepover duty," he said, and popped off the lid for me.

I drank straight from the bottle. "I'm glad I only have one child. No way could I have handled more."

He chuckled. "Give yourself credit, Rose. You've done a remarkable job with the one you do have. Not every parent can say that and have it be true."

"I can't take credit for Marley," I said. "She'd be this awesome even if she'd hatched fully formed from the head of a Gorgon."

He squinted at me. "You've got some weird thoughts. You know that?"

"I assumed it was one of the things you like about me." I took another sip of ale.

He placed his hand on my thigh. It felt warm and inviting resting there. "I like an awful things about you, Rose." He leaned back and removed his hand. "Not so sure about the weird thoughts, though."

I nudged him away with my foot. "Not funny, Granger. I have feelings, you know. Weird feelings, but still."

He laughed. "You're such an easy target."

The kitchen door flew open and Marley stood there with a necklace hanging from her hand. "Mom, you have to see this locket. It's the prettiest thing in the world." She came to stand beside me and proudly displayed the gold necklace with the locket in the shape of a heart. Inside the locket was a tiny picture of Karl on one side and a tiny picture of me on the other.

"Where did you get this?" I asked, stunned.

"Sheriff Nash," Marley said. "Thank you so much. I love it." She kissed the locket and ran back to the living area.

My chest ached. "You gave Marley a locket with a photo of her dad?"

"And you," he said. "Don't forget the most important part."

I gazed at him in wonder. "How did you get your hands on a photo of Karl?"

He smiled vaguely. "I'm the sheriff. I have my ways." He took a swig of ale. "I know what it's like to lose a father. I figure it's only right that Marley keeps his memory close to her heart."

Emotions swelled inside me and I realized that I was on the verge of tears. I pushed back my chair and stood, but the sheriff shot to his feet and grabbed my hand before I could turn away.

"Where're you going, Rose?" His voice was more tender than usual.

I swallowed hard. "I have something in my eye."

He lifted my chin. "Those are called tears, Rose, and they're a perfectly acceptable display of emotion."

A lone tear streamed down my cheek and he dabbed it gently with the pad of his finger.

"Mom, look at this!" Marley pushed open the door and I quickly pulled myself together.

"What is it?" There was no need to ask. I could see what it was.

A wand.

"We'll to have to stay up past midnight so I can use it," Marley said.

"Who bought you the wand?" I asked.

"Aunt Hyacinth," she replied. "She didn't buy it, though. It's a family heirloom. At least that's what her note said."

I examined the wand in her hand. With its well-worn groove marks and runes along the handle, it definitely looked ancient.

"That's a nice stick you're holding," the sheriff said. "Why don't you put it somewhere safe until you're ready to use it? You'd never forgive yourself if anything happened to it."

Marley's expression turned solemn. "You're so right." She held the wand up to me. "Will you take care of it for me?"

"Of course." I took the wand and, the moment Marley left the kitchen, I gave the wand to the sheriff. "You're probably better at keeping things safe."

He chuckled. "I'll find a good hiding spot." He studied the wand. "Hyacinth must be pretty confident the girl's going to be a witch."

"Hudson and Bryn were disappointing to her, but werewolf genes can apparently be strong," I said. "Human genes… well." I shrugged. "I think she can't imagine a world where garden-variety human genes overpower the DNA of the One True Witch."

He sidled up to me. "Werewolf genes *are* pretty potent. In fact, I'd say everything about a werewolf is pretty potent."

I placed my palm flat against his forehead. "Down, boy."

He gripped my fingers and kissed them. "I'll go in any direction you like when the time comes. Werewolves are flexible."

My body warmed all over. "Hold that thought for another night. It's time to get these girls some birthday cake."

CHAPTER TEN

SUNDAY WAS NOT a good day in Rose Cottage. Once her friends had gone home, Marley moped around the house as though she'd been diagnosed with a terminal illness. I honestly didn't know how to make her feel better. There was nothing I could do to change the outcome and she'd already had pizza and cake. In my experience, those were the food choices that improved my outlook on life.

"Do you want to go to the beach after my psychic skills lesson with Marigold?" I asked. Marley loved the beach more than anyone I knew. If that suggestion didn't perk her up, nothing would.

"Not in the mood," she said sullenly. She fell backward on the sofa and folded her arms. I noticed that she wore the heart-shaped locket around her neck.

"I'm so impressed with Granger's gift," I said, coming to sit beside her. "It's beautiful."

Marley fingered the locket. "It is. I like that he included Dad."

"He lost his father at a young age, too," I said. "He understands what it's like."

Marley cast a sidelong glance at me. "Do you want to marry him?"

"Marry him?" I sputtered. "Let's not get ahead of ourselves. We've only recently decided to step forward with the relationship. Besides, I'm not sure whether I'd ever get married again."

"Don't you want a companion for when I go off to college?" She placed her hands over the dog's ears. "PP3 isn't going to live forever."

"You turned eleven yesterday," I said. "I have plenty of time for major life decisions between now and then."

She exhaled loudly. "Maybe you should settle down with a nice wizard to appease Aunt Hyacinth. Now that I'm a boring human, she might not be as generous as she has been."

"Oh, Marley, don't say that. Aunt Hyacinth isn't as rigid as she pretends to be."

"What makes you think that?" Marley asked.

"I think Hattie's death is giving her pause," I said. "She seems to be softening her stance on a few things."

"Did she give you and the sheriff her blessing?" Marley asked. "It has to be hard for her because she dislikes Wyatt so much."

"Wyatt didn't treat Linnea very well," I said, not wanting to get into details about his cheating ways. "He and Granger aren't at all similar."

"But Aunt Hyacinth dislikes him because he's a werewolf above all else."

I rubbed my hands on my thighs. "Yeah, you're probably right."

"She adores Alec, though," Marley said. "So at least we agree on something."

I ruffled her hair. "You're still holding out hope for that one, aren't you? He's with Holly now. You know that."

"It won't last," Marley said. "She's not right for him."

"You're very wise, sweetheart, but I don't think you can say whether Holly and Alec are meant to be." I smiled. "On that note, I asked Aunt Hyacinth if she intended to start dating anytime soon."

Marley burst into laughter. "You what?"

"Why is that funny? She's an attractive older witch with money and power. She'd have her choice of decent men."

Marley's eyes sparkled with excitement. "We should send her to see Artemis. Maybe she can find Aunt Hyacinth the perfect match. If she's happy in her own relationship, maybe she'll stay out of others'."

"That's not a bad idea," I said. PP3 jumped off the sofa and I knew that Marigold had arrived. "Do you want to quietly observe the lesson?"

Marley peeled herself off the sofa. "No, thanks. What's the point? I'll go read Alec's book in my room."

I felt deflated. Any other time, Marley would have jumped at the chance to watch a magic lesson. "We'll be in here if you change your mind." I'd make sure we conducted the lesson in the cottage rather than the woods today, so that I could stay close to Marley. I didn't want to leave her alone.

I opened the door and was confronted with a giant stuffed black cat. Marigold peered around it. "Where's the birthday girl?"

"Upstairs," I said. "She isn't feeling very festive."

Marigold crossed the threshold and set aside the cat. "No magic?" she whispered.

"Afraid not."

Marigold frowned. "Has she been seen by anyone?"

"Well, of course. She's not a ghost."

Marigold narrowed her eyes. "I mean a professional."

"A professional what?"

"A healer. A therapist. Someone to help figure out whether this is a blockage or a permanent condition."

I stared at her. "A blockage? Is that a thing?"

Marigold shrugged. "Everything's a thing."

I hesitated. "I don't want to give her false hope. She's already devastated."

"Then she won't get any more devastated," Marigold said. "I can recommend a therapist. A friend of mine sees him regularly and swears by him."

What harm could it do? "I'll take his information and see what Marley thinks."

"Rhys Meridien," she said. "He has an office over on Blue Moon Lane."

"Thanks," I said. "How's the change?" I dropped my voice to a whisper.

"Why are you whispering?" Marigold asked, mimicking my voice.

"Because I don't know if you want to anyone to know," I replied.

"Well, I don't intend to lease a billboard, but it's a natural part of life," Marigold said. "Nothing to be embarrassed about."

"That's such a healthy attitude," I said. "Did that happen as part of the change?"

She glowered at me. "I'm a perfectly together witch, Ember. I make no apologies."

"Blargh. You're no fun," I said. "Where's Hazel when I need an emotional punching bag?"

A noise in the kitchen drew my attention. "I'll be right back." I opened the kitchen door and found Raoul scraping the icing off the edge of the cake box. I stood there with my hands on my hips until he noticed me.

What? he finally said, indignant. *I'm not allowed to partake? I'm family.*

"You've managed to cover your face in icing," I said.

That's for later. He gestured toward the front of the

cottage. *I come bearing gifts. Where's the witch? Let me know when her familiar makes an appearance so I can show him the ropes.*

I pressed my lips together. This whole ordeal was going to take a toll on Marley and me. I felt guilty having to explain to everyone that—no, Marley seems to have inherited her father's non-magic DNA.

Raoul's dark eyes rounded. *No transformation?*

I shook my head. "I'm sure she'll take the present, though."

It's on the lawn, he said.

I went to the window and peered outside. "Raoul, why is there a refrigerator on my front lawn?"

Ta-da! You're welcome.

"What did you…Raoul, is this from a dumpster?"

How insulting! I found it in the fresh pile at the recycling center. Hasn't even been rained on yet.

"How did you manage to get it here?" I shook my head. "Never mind. I don't want to know." I stared at the massive refrigerator. "What are those red marks? Paint?"

Raoul took a sudden interest in the floorboards. *I may have been involved in a scuffle to take ownership of this. There were a few others interested. It's a big-ticket item, you know.*

I was touched, and yet completely grossed out. "You got in a fight over Marley's present?"

I didn't want to miss the opportunity to get something nice. Now that I know about the magic, I'm glad I made the effort.

Marigold poked her head in the kitchen. "Ember, are you coming back?" She caught sight of my familiar. "Ah, Raoul. You may as well join us. This is psychic skills, after all."

Raoul rolled his eyes. *Why didn't you tell me the Nazi cheerleader was here?*

"Is he rolling his eyes at me? He is, isn't he?" Marigold scowled.

"Hey, he prefers you to Hazel," I said.

That seemed to perk up Marigold. "I see." She beamed at the raccoon. "Come then, let's get on with the lesson. I have other boxes to tick today."

We returned to the living area and sat around the larger table. Marigold had a small basket of items in the middle.

Awesome. Treasures. Raoul settled into a chair and reached for the basket, but Marigold slapped his paw away.

"These can only be touched by Ember or the lesson won't work," Marigold said. She gave the basket a gentle shake. "Close your eyes and draw a single item from the pile."

I did as instructed, wrapping my fingers around something small and wooden. "Do I look at it?"

"Not yet," Marigold said. "Best to keep your eyes shut, so that your other senses kick in more quickly."

"Am I supposed to guess what it is?" That seemed…not very interesting.

"No," Marigold replied. "I'd like you to focus on the energy emanating from the object. How does it make you feel? Do you have any thoughts or impressions while you're holding the object?"

I sat quietly for a moment, rubbing my fingers over the item. At first, my rational mind kept trying to figure out what it was, rather than how it made me feel. Finally, I cleared my mind and zeroed in on the energy.

"Sad," I said. "I'm feeling a sad energy."

"Stick with it." Marigold fell silent for a moment. "Anything else? Any visions?"

I stroked the wooden object, concentrating as hard as I could on the vibrations rolling off the item. "Someone lost this…No, wait. Someone hid this away because the memories attached to it were too painful." In my mind's eye, I saw blurred figures but nothing more.

"Very good, Ember," Marigold said. "You may open your eyes now."

I immediately glanced down at the object. It was a fairly plain, smooth piece of wood. "What is it?" And why would it bring such sadness to anyone?

"A handmade teething rattle," Marigold said. "The infant died before she was ever able to use it. Her father had carved it especially for her."

Tears threatened to spill as I stared at the beautiful piece. "Why do you have it?"

"The mother is a friend," Marigold replied. "Years ago, she asked me to take this out of the house so that they were no longer reminded of their loss. Of course, removing an object will never be enough to erase the painful memories."

I placed the teething rattle back in the basket. "There's still a lot of sadness attached to it."

Marigold nodded solemnly. "Energy can cling to an item for its lifetime. That's one reason psychometry is such a useful skill to hone."

"That's what this lesson is?" I asked. "Psychometry?"

"Yes." She removed the wooden teething rattle and shook the basket. "Another one, please. Make sure the first one wasn't a lucky guess."

I closed my eyes and pulled another object from the basket. This time, I didn't try to discern what it was, only noting that it was circular. I tried to simply focus on the energy. The vibrations felt—almost hot to the touch.

"Anger?" I said.

"Are you asking me or telling me?" Marigold asked.

I sat with the item another minute. "Telling you. There's anger attached to this item."

"Can you tell anything about the being connected to it?" Marigold asked. "Male or female?"

I inhaled deeply through my nose and exhaled through

110

my mouth. "The owner of the object was female, but the anger is masculine, if that makes sense."

"Yes, it does. Any visions?"

I squeezed my eyes, as though that might somehow prompt a clear vision. It didn't. "Just blurry figures."

"That will come in time," Marigold said. "You have the capability, I'm certain of it."

"Can I open my eyes?"

"You may."

I uncurled my fingers and saw the ring in my hand. "A bad marriage?"

"A called-off engagement," Marigold said. "He tried to kill her. Thankfully, a couple of bystanders intervened."

I tossed the ring at Marigold, not wanting anything to do with it. "I'm already having an emotionally charged weekend, Marigold. Any chance we can pep things up?"

"That depends on the object you choose," she said. "Unfortunately, negative emotions have a way of sticking around for longer and giving off stronger vibrations."

You're pretty good at this, Raoul said.

I glared at him from across the table. "Don't sound so surprised."

Can I do it, too? he asked. *Ask the Nazi cheerleader.*

Only if you refer to her by her name.

Oh, you mean the way you refer to Hazel as the crazed clown?

I huffed. "Marigold, Raoul would like to know whether he's capable of psychometry, too?"

Marigold looked contemplatively at the raccoon. "Do you know what? I'm not entirely sure. He can read your thoughts of an object, of course, but I don't know whether he can pick up the energy on his own." She pushed the basket in his direction. "Why don't you try? It can't do any harm."

Raoul placed one paw over his eyes and used the other

paw to fish through the items in the basket. He pulled a chewed bone from the pile and tapped his claws against it.

Hey, I think I got a happy one. He stuck out his tongue at me. *Take that, Saddy McSadness.*

"He says his object is thoroughly depressing," I said.

Marigold's brow rose. "Really?"

I blew out a breath. "No. He says he feels happiness."

"Well." Marigold seemed to relax. "That makes more sense. Anything else?"

Raoul held the bone against his body. *Contentment. Whoever owned this felt like he had a good, full life.*

I repeated his words to Marigold and her lips curved into a smile. "I suppose it's a shared gift after all. Open your eyes, Raoul."

He took note of the bone. *How about that? A dog?*

"A dog?" I said aloud.

"That's right," Marigold said. "His name was, unimaginatively, Rover. He died of natural causes after a long and happy life."

Yeah, I got that. Raoul looked at me. *It felt weird to experience emotions that don't belong to you or me.*

You mean it felt weird to experience happiness and contentment.

He shot me a menacing look.

"One more round," Marigold said. "Then I need to head off. It is Sunday, you know. I only do this because her ladyship requires it."

Raoul snickered. *Her ladyship. She's talking about your uppity aunt.*

"Yes, Raoul. I know perfectly well who she's talking about." I closed my eyes and reached forward. A cylindrical wooden object slid into my hand. I pushed aside the thoughts associated with the physical properties in order to access the energy. My chest tightened and I could hardly breathe from the onslaught of feelings. Emotions flooded me—good and bad. Fear, pain, happiness, desperation.

"What is it, Ember?" Marigold asked. "Do you see anything?"

I focused on my mind's eye and an image of a woman appeared in shadow. She wasn't blurry like previous images, but I still couldn't see much of her—not even the color of her hair. The energy, on the other hand, was overwhelming.

"I see a woman," I said. "I feel strength and power and disappointment." I paused to catch my breath. "Any emotion you can name, I'm probably feeling it right now."

"Fascinating," Marigold whispered. "You may let go it now. Wouldn't want to risk upsetting your aunt by shocking your system."

I blinked open my eyes. "Am I right?"

Marigold shrugged. "I can only assume so. I didn't bring this object with me. It was the wand that was left out, presumably from Marley's birthday party."

I gaped at the ancient wand. "Yes, it was a gift from Aunt Hyacinth."

"Sounds like there's a story there," she said. "A lot of stories, in fact."

I scrutinized the wand more closely. "More than I could have possibly imagined."

CHAPTER ELEVEN

DEPUTY BOLAN and I stood on the front step of Avonne and Stone's beautiful brick house. Every flower and shrub seemed carefully chosen and the yard was landscaped within an inch of its life. I waited patiently for the leprechaun to knock, letting him take the lead so that he didn't get his green panties in a twist. After an uncomfortable silence, he cleared his throat.

"What's the holdup, Deputy Bolan?" I asked.

His gaze shifted to the door. "There's no doorbell."

"And?" It took me another beat before I made the connection. "Oh!" He couldn't reach the knocker on the door. "Allow me." I gripped the brass ring and banged it against the door.

"You're enjoying this, aren't you?" Deputy Bolan asked, his arms folded.

"I love knocking on doors," I said. "Reminds me of trick-or-treating in my youth."

"Liar."

The door cracked open and Avonne's pretty face appeared in the gap. "Ember, what a surprise."

"You remember Deputy Bolan from Rollins Manor," I said. I moved aside so that she could get a better view of the leprechaun. "We'd like to talk to you about your grandmother, if you don't mind."

"Of course." She widened the gap and we stepped inside the house. The interior was as organized and tasteful as the outside. "The children are at school, so I was taking the opportunity to work on my designs." She walked toward an open room to the right of the foyer where a conference room-length table was pushed against the wall.

"Designs for what?" I asked.

"I've been hoping to start a clothing line," she said. "Stone spends so much of his time at work. Now that the kids are in school full-time, I need a focus of my own. I can only serve on the board of so many charitable organizations before it all feels the same."

I glanced at the table where dozens of sketches were spread out in a neat row. "These are gorgeous," I said. They were dress designs in varying lengths and styles.

"Do you really think so?" Avonne sat in the chair at the table and picked up the nearest sketch. "Fashion is my passion. I even like that as a company tagline."

"It's good," I said. "You should be proud of these."

Avonne frowned. "I wish my family agreed with you. They would rather mock me than support me."

"Really?" I said. "That's a shame."

Avonne leaned her chin on the open palm of her hand. "I suppose I'm being overly dramatic. They just don't approve of a clothing line. They think it doesn't fit with our family's image."

"By 'they,' do you mean your grandmother?" I asked.

She looked up at me and smiled. "Basically. I asked for seed money to start the business and she refused."

Deputy Bolan and I exchanged glances. At least she was

being forthcoming about that fact. Of course, she was probably smart enough to realize that we already knew and it was the reason for our visit.

"She thought the Rollins-Mahoney clan was too fancy for a clothing line?" the deputy asked. "Because a clothing line sounds fancy to me."

Avonne tapped the paper in front of her. "It's not that simple. We're a wealthy family, Deputy Bolan. We don't have jobs in the traditional sense. Stone is enough of an anomaly, but he's excused because he married into our family rather than being born into it."

"Your grandmother didn't want you to have careers?" I asked.

"She had very specific ideas about what we could and could not do with our lives," Avonne said. "After our parents died, she became even more adamant. Apparently, she'd advised against the yacht and they'd bought it anyway." She stared at the drawing of the dress in front of her. "I think she secretly blamed herself for their deaths, for not putting her foot down about the yacht, and took her guilt out on the rest of us."

"That must have been difficult," I said.

"Yes, it was," Avonne said. "I was told who I was permitted to marry, which organizations I was allowed to join, which friends I could have." A single tear dripped from cheek to the paper, creating a smudge on the image of the dress.

"Did you ever speak to your grandmother about your discontent?" Deputy Bolan asked.

Avonne snorted. "I tried many times, but Grandmother was extremely stubborn."

"But you chose Stone, didn't you?" I asked. I didn't get the sense that she'd been forced to marry him.

"Oh, absolutely," Avonne said. "I was fortunate that Grandmother approved, or we could have ended up like my sister and Weston." She clucked her tongue. "What a mess that whole thing was."

"And you don't like mess, do you?" I asked. The state of her house alone was indicative of that.

"Definitely not," Avonne replied.

"So what happens now that your grandmother is dead?" the deputy asked. "Will you be able to use your inheritance to fund your new business?"

"Yes, my share will easily fund the business," she said.

"Did you know that before the reading of the will?" I asked.

"I knew that I would inherit," Avonne said. "I've always been a good girl and caved to Grandmother's demands, not like Lacey."

So Hattie refused to fund her granddaughter's business, and Avonne knew she'd inherit enough money from the estate to cover her startup costs. I smelled a strong motive.

"I understand you had breakfast alone with your grandmother the morning of her party," I said.

"Yes." She exhaled softly. "The last time I'll ever spend alone with her. It seems surreal."

"Did the two of you get along?" the deputy asked. "Any arguments that morning?"

"Nobody got along with Grandmother," Avonne said. "Not really. She was too ornery. I did try to please her, though. For better or worse, it's in my nature to be a pleaser." She offered a sad smile. "My husband accuses me of it all the time. He wants me to please him, of course, but he's not so keen on everyone else."

"You must've resented Hattie for not letting you pursue your dream," I said.

Avonne picked up a pencil and began a fresh sketch. "Maybe at first, but I got over it. Having Stone has been a blessing. He keeps me grounded and Grandmother liked him well enough, which made my life easier. It bumped me up the pecking order anyway."

"Above Lacey, I guess," I said.

"Yes, and Ella," Avonne replied. "Not Fitz, though. He was Grandmother's favorite. I swore that was the reason he refused to get involved in a serious relationship. He worried too much about losing her approval if Grandmother disliked the woman."

"If you and Fitz were favored over Ella, why does Ella get the house?" I asked.

Avonne appeared unconcerned. "Neither of us wanted the house, but Ella's more than happy to take it on. Personally, my memories of growing up there aren't full of rainbows and unicorns. Anyway, it's expensive to maintain, as you can imagine."

"Can you think of anyone with a reason to kill your grandmother?" Deputy Bolan asked.

Avonne shrugged. "Anyone she ever met?" She laughed bitterly. "Like I said, nobody got along with Grandmother. Of course, that doesn't generally lead to murder, so it's hard to say."

"Thanks for your help, Avonne," I said. "Best of luck with your design business. If it means anything, I'd totally wear one of those dresses."

Avonne beamed at me. "Thank you, Ember. Actually, it means everything to me."

Marley and I sat in the office of Rhys Meridien, awaiting our appointment. I had no idea what to expect from Marigold's suggested therapist. Marley had been eager to come and see whether the druid could help unlock the magic she was still convinced she possessed. I was of two minds. Mostly, I didn't want to make matters worse by dragging out the inevitable.

The door to Rhys's office opened and my mouth dropped open. "Lacey?" The morgen was quickly followed by Weston. It didn't escape my notice that they were holding hands.

Lacey's cheeks colored. "Ember! I didn't expect to see anyone I know here."

I didn't know how to respond. It seemed rude to ask probing questions about the exes' relationship.

Weston squeezed her hand. "Now that the old windbag is out of our lives, Lacey and I have decided to give us another shot. The only way Lacey would agree was if I went to couples counseling." He smiled at her. "So here we are."

"I guess Grandmother's death isn't all doom and gloom," Lacey said. "I'll have a nice inheritance and my husband back." She inclined her head. "How's the investigation coming along anyway? I can't get my money until the murderer is caught."

"You'd have to ask the sheriff," I said. As far as I knew, Lacey was still on the shortlist. After all, she was the only one with a version of the accelerant in her possession.

"Miss Rose?" A man's head poked into the waiting area. "Ready when you are."

Marley and I rose to our feet. "Good luck with everything, Lacey," I said.

"Thanks." She eyed Weston. "I'm sure I need it."

Marley and I entered the druid's office and I began to inspect the diplomas on the wall. Rhys Meridien was a certified healer, as well as a certified counselor.

"I heal the mind and the body," Rhys said, as though reading my mind. "A holistic approach."

Marley and I squished together on the settee, while Rhys sat across from us in a wingback chair. He reminded me of Santa Claus, with white hair and a fluffy white beard to match. His round stomach suggested lots of pot roasts and very little exercise.

"What's my role here?" I asked. "Do I sit as an active participant? Lurk awkwardly in the background?"

The therapist looked at Marley. "That's up to you. You call the shots in this room, Marley."

I wagged a finger. "As long as they're not Jell-O shots." My cheeks flamed. "Sorry, that's a human world reference and not appropriate for children." I had no idea how to behave in a therapist's office. I felt completely out of my depth.

"You don't need to be nervous, Miss Rose," the therapist said. "You aren't on trial. We're simply having a conversation."

I fidgeted in my seat. "I'm not nervous."

"I'm the anxious one," Marley said. "Mom is always cool and collected...unless she's cooking. Or driving. Or...."

"Okay, thank you, Marley," I said.

The therapist bit back a smile. "What makes you believe you're the anxious one, Marley?"

"Because Mom always says so," she replied.

My jaw hit the floor. "Based on this little thing called *evidence*."

The therapist folded his hands on the hill that doubled as his stomach. "What kind of evidence, Miss Rose?"

"Where do I start? Her mind races all the time with every possible bad outcome to a situation. She always had to sleep with me until we moved here," I said. "She still comes into my room in the middle of the night sometimes."

The therapist glanced at Marley. "Is this accurate?"

Marley hedged slightly. "Yes."

"She doesn't like heights," I said. "I took her broomstick riding and I thought she was going to leave scars around my abdomen."

"Heights are a common fear, Miss Rose." He shifted his attention back to Marley. "When did you start co-sleeping with your mother?"

"After my dad died."

"I see." The therapist jotted down a few notes. "And his death was unexpected?"

"Yes, he…" I began to explain, but the therapist held up a hand. "This is the part where you lurk awkwardly in the background."

"Sure. I can do that." I pretended to zip my lip.

"He died in an accident," Marley said. "After that, I was afraid of losing my mom, too, so I wanted to be as close to her as possible when she was around."

My heart melted. "Marley…."

The therapist gave me a pointed look and I snapped my mouth shut.

"And what made you feel comfortable enough to scale back the number of nights you slept in her bed?" he asked.

Marley plucked a loose thread on the hem of her shirt. "I don't know. I guess when our cousins came to rescue us in our apartment. They were so confident…fierce." She smiled. "I started to feel safe in Starry Hollow, like nothing bad could happen to us because we're magical and powerful—or, at least, my family is."

"You know that's an illusion, though, right?" he asked.

"Um, excuse me?" I said. "Aren't we supposed to encourage the whole feeling safe thing? Can we please not talk her out of it?"

The therapist chuckled. "What's your job, Miss Rose?"

"She's a reporter for *Vox Populi*," Marley said. I felt a surge of affection upon hearing the note of pride in her voice. What I did mattered to her. It was both heartening and a bit scary, that sense of responsibility.

"Let's come to an understanding right from then start," the therapist said. "I won't tell you how to write your articles for the paper and you don't tell me how to conduct my therapy sessions. Do we have a deal?"

"Yes, sir," I mumbled. Apparently, I was not as good at awkwardly lurking as I believed.

"And how have you settled into school?" he asked. "Have you made friends? Grades are good?"

"Yes, but I'd really like to attend the Black Cloak Academy," she said. "That only happens if I come into my magic, though. That's a requirement to go there."

"And why is this so important to you?" he asked. "Your mother didn't attend there, did she?"

I suppressed a laugh. My life would have turned out much differently if I'd lived in Starry Hollow with full knowledge of my heritage. I would never have met Karl and Marley would never have been born. I shuddered to think about it.

"I'm a Rose," Marley said. "Roses attend the Black Cloak Academy."

"Your cousins, Bryn and Hudson," the therapist began, "they are Roses, are they not?"

Marley pulled harder on the loose thread. "Yes."

"But they don't attend there, do they?"

"No, because their werewolf genes were dominant," Marley said.

"What do you think will happen if you become a witch?" he asked. "Will your life be better somehow?"

"Of course!" Her whole face lit up. "Magic makes everything better. If I have magic, I'll be able to handle scary situations. If my mom had had magic years ago, instead of it being suppressed, maybe she could have saved my dad."

Great Goddess of the Moon. "Marley, I wasn't even there when he died. My magic couldn't have saved him."

"And that would be an awful lot of responsibility, wouldn't it?" Rhys asked. "When things do go wrong...If those you love do get hurt, then would you blame yourself, even when events are out of your control?"

Marley stared into her lap. "Maybe."

"How does that make you feel?" he asked.

Marley laughed. "Anxious." She glanced at me. "I guess you're right, as always."

"It's okay, Marley. I don't need to be right," I said.

Marley fixed her gaze on me. "Don't you?"

"What does that mean?"

"Isn't that why you can't decide whether to go all in with the sheriff?" she asked. "That you might be wrong. That maybe you should've chosen Alec."

My stomach tightened. "This is your therapy session, Marley, not mine."

"You're very astute for your age, aren't you?" Rhys asked her.

"Yes," Marley said.

"That combination of intellectual and emotional intelligence at a young age…" He whistled. "It can be torture on an undeveloped brain."

"Can you help her?" I asked. "If there really is some kind of blockage, can you…plumb it?"

He laughed. "Rhys Meridien, emotional plumber. I like it." He extended his hands to Marley. "Would you mind joining hands for a moment, Marley? This is where the traditional druid healing practices come into play."

Marley held his hands. I observed silently as Rhys closed his eyes and concentrated.

"It feels like little sparks of electricity," Marley said. She didn't seem uncomfortable.

"I'm trying to help open you up, if that is, indeed, the problem," Rhys said. He opened his eyes and released her hands.

"What did you feel?" I asked.

Rhys placed his hands on his thighs. "This young woman carries an awful lot inside that small body," he replied.

"An awful lot of magic?" Marley asked hopefully.

"I can't be sure," Rhys said. "I'm sorry. Let's meet again soon, and see if we can't work toward a breakthrough."

"But what if there's nothing to break through?" I asked.

He gave me a knowing look. "I'm not only talking about magic, Miss Rose. Your daughter has a lot of emotions to manage. Either way, I think she'll benefit from our conversations."

"I'd like to try, Mom," Marley said. "I know you don't want to give me false hope, but that's not how I see it. Like Mr. Meridien said, it's an opportunity to work through all these complex emotions."

Well, if Marley wanted to try, then I wasn't going to stand in her way. "Okay, Mr. Meridien. I guess we'll see you next time."

He eyed me closely. "You should think about making an appointment for yourself, too, Miss Rose. I don't even have to hold your hands to sense your complex emotions."

I bristled. "I'm good, thanks."

Rhys gave me a patient smile. "Your choice, but you know where to find me if you ever change your mind."

CHAPTER TWELVE

I SAILED into the Caffeinated Cauldron, intending to dart in and out. I'd almost made it to the exit when the sight of a certain nymph at a table by the window stopped me in my tracks.

"Holly?" I said.

The nymph whipped around and I immediately noticed the mascara streaks under her eyes. "Ember." She fished a tissue from her purse and dabbed at the makeup. "Sorry, I sneezed and now my makeup is a mess."

I pretended to buy her story. "Everything good with you?"

"Getting there," she said. "I had a rough patch where I didn't feel like myself, but I'm back to normal now. Mostly."

"Rough in what way?" I asked. Although I didn't want to pry, it felt rude not to ask a follow-up question.

She stuffed the tissue back in her pocket. "Just off. You know how it is. I had a moody spell, which is so unlike me. I'm always upbeat."

I didn't dare ask about Alec's place in all this. It was none of my business. None. At. All. "I'm glad you're feeling better."

"Are you busy? Do you want to sit down and have coffee with me?" She held up her cup.

My stomach twisted. Why did she have to be so nice? "I would love to, but I'm jetting in and out. I'm heading over to interview one of Hattie Rollins-Mahoney's relatives."

Her face crumpled. "Oh, that poor morgen. Alec told me about her. Two hundred years old and murdered by a member of her own family? How awful."

"We don't know yet whether it was a relative," I said. "There's at least one member of staff on the suspect list as well."

Holly squeezed my arm. "It must be so traumatic, covering stories like this one. You really are forced to see the worst in others."

"The article was meant to be all about Hattie's party for the society section," I said. "I didn't intend to cover a murder."

"Alec said you have a way of getting to the bottom of things." She cocked her head, thinking. "Pretty sure the word he used was tenacious." She giggled in that girlish way she had. "He said you're like a vampire with her fangs in a good vein."

"What else does he say?" The question slipped out and I wished I could snatch it back. What did it matter what Alec told his girlfriend about me?

Holly twisted a tendril around her finger. "He thinks you have the capacity to be an excellent reporter and that you're a better writer than he expected, given your background."

"Wow, that's a pretty big compliment coming from him," I said. "Would be nice to hear that from him directly once in a blood moon."

"I know how you feel," Holly said. "He isn't very forthcoming with compliments." She chewed her lip. "Or any sort of thoughts, feelings, or emotions." She laughed. "Oh, that sounds terrible. Alec is amazing."

"He's something," I said vaguely.

"He talks about you a lot, actually. A more insecure girl might even be jealous." In an unexpected move, she reached out and pinched my cheek. "But I know you and the sheriff are hot and heavy. That werewolf is devoted to you. I wish Alec looked at me the way Sheriff Nash looks at you."

My pulse quickened. "Really?"

"Honey, I would give both boobs for that kind of pure adoration." She paused. "Okay, maybe not the whole boobs. A few cups."

I couldn't resist a smile. As much as I wanted to dislike her, Holly had an endearing quality that appealed to me.

"Maybe we could meet for coffee later this week?" she suggested. Her expression of hope made me want to pour the hot latte all over my head. I didn't deserve her friendship. Not when part of me secretly rooted for her relationship to fail. I was a horrible person. Here I had the sheriff's 'adoration,' and yet I still yearned for Alec's attention. How greedy could one woman be? Complex emotions, indeed, Mr. Meridien.

"I'll check my schedule and get back to you."

She flashed a grateful smile. "Terrific. Good luck with your article."

I exited the coffee shop and drove to the Rollins-Mahoney estate, guzzling down my latte on the way. I drove past the main house to the back border of the property where Ella's house was nestled in a clearing. While it wasn't as quaint as Rose Cottage, the gingerbread-style house certainly had charm and character. I noticed Ella outside pruning some of the bushes in the front. Okay, clearly this was where our similarities deviated. Plants and flowers in my care had basically signed their death warrants.

I stepped out of the car and smiled. "Good morning, Ella."

"Oh, hello," she said, shielding her eyes from the sun. "I wasn't expecting any visitors. I wouldn't have put on my grubby clothes."

Her idea of grubby clothes was a pretty floral blouse and neatly pressed shorts. The morgen was far more stylish than I was.

"I thought the estate had a gardener," I said. With all the acreage here, it seemed impossible not to.

"We do, but Aunt Hattie would never let him include my plot in his tasks," Ella said. "She wanted me to be solely responsible for its upkeep."

I surveyed the plot surrounding the house. There were fruit trees, bushes, and flowerbeds, not to mention the grass itself. "That's a lot of work, even if you enjoy it."

"I had to prove myself, you see," Ella said. She removed her bright pink gardening gloves and set them on a tree stump. "Would you like to come inside for a drink?"

"I don't want to interrupt your work," I said. "I only wanted to ask a few questions for the article I'm writing about Hattie."

"I'm surprised they've decided to run it anyway," Ella said. "The society articles are generally upbeat. This one doesn't end very well."

I declined to tell her the article was now focused on the murder. I wanted her to feel free to say whatever was on her mind. "I could help you here. We can talk while we"—I glanced around—"do whatever it is you're doing."

Her expression brightened. It seemed as though she wasn't offered help very often. "Let me grab you another pair of pruning shears," she said. "I'll be right back."

It would be like handing scissors to a pigeon. She was so enthusiastic, though, that I didn't want to disappoint her. I'd handle those shears like a pro—or at least I'd pretend to.

"Apologies in advance," I whispered to the greenery around me.

"Here you go." Ella hurried back and handed me a purple pair of shears. She loved her bright colors.

"Thanks." I watched how Ella positioned hers before I made a move. No need to flaunt my ignorance. "So how was the reading of the will? That happened recently, didn't it?" Although I knew the contents of the will, I wanted to hear Ella's version of events.

She scowled and clipped with extra intensity. "Yes, but the whole thing is ridiculous. No distributions can be made until they've apprehended the murderer."

I cast her a sidelong glance. "Aren't *you* interested in having your aunt's murderer brought to justice? I would think that's a priority."

Her cheeks grew flushed. "Of course. I didn't mean it that way. It's just that I was promised the deed to the main house. That's part of proving myself with the care of this smaller house. I've earned it."

"What about her grandchildren?" I asked. Would her story match Avonne's?

Her lips formed a straight line. "They weren't interested in the house. They'll get plenty of money. The house was promised to me."

"And is that what the will said?" I asked.

"Yes, except I can't take possession until this whole mess is resolved." She scaled back the rapidity of her clipping. "I'm not even convinced she was murdered."

I dropped the shears to my side. "There was a potion found in her system that she wasn't taking. An accelerant that caused her to have a heart attack. The autopsy report suggests it was mixed in with her mead. How is that not murder?"

Ella lowered her gaze. "I don't know. I just can't see what

129

anyone would have to gain at this point by murdering her. She would've only lasted a couple more years. What was the rush?"

"That's the point of the investigation," I said. "Maybe someone needed their share of the money sooner rather than later. Maybe your aunt pushed someone too far with he acerbic personality."

Ella snorted. "In that case, we'd all be responsible for her death."

"Why did she promise you the house specifically?" I asked.

Ella sighed. "Because the house should have gone to my grandfather, her older brother. He died before their parents, though, so the house went to Aunt Hattie. I think she's always felt guilty over that, though she'd never admit it. So this was her way of setting things right in the family."

"But her grandchildren have children," I said. "What if you don't leave any heirs? What will happen to the house?"

Ella straightened. "I have every intention of marrying and having children. I'm still young and, as Aunt Hattie proved, morgens can live long lives."

"Are you dating anyone now?" I asked.

She shook her head. "I was always afraid of courting Aunt Hattie's disapproval and getting written out of the will, so I avoided men. Now that she's passed, though, I plan to get out there. My clock's been ticking for years."

I felt a pang of sympathy for Ella. Like Fitz, she feared her aunt's disapproval so much that she was willing to put her entire life on hold. That would never have been me. No house was worth the price. Then again, maybe Ella got tired of waiting and living a life alone. Maybe she wanted to hurry along her aunt's demise.

"I know a good matchmaker in town, if you're interested," I said. "Artemis Haverford."

Ella broke into an enthusiastic smile. "Yes, I've heard she's very good. I was planning to try the old-fashioned way first."

"And what's that?"

She laughed. "Bars."

"Steer clear of my cousin, Florian, if you meet him," I said. "He's not the settling-down type."

"So he's like Fitzgerald," Ella said.

"Sort of. What's your impression of Sampson?" I asked. "He's the only one with a key to the mead cellar aside from Hattie. Do you think he's capable of killing your aunt? I can't imagine it was an easy job, being her servant."

Ella moved to a different section and resumed pruning. "Sampson is the sweetest man on the planet. He has a no-kill policy for insects, so I can't believe he wouldn't extend that policy to paranormals."

"You feel like you know him well?" I asked.

"We spend a lot of time together," she said. "In fact, we had tea together the day before the party."

"Here?" I didn't think Hattie would take kindly to the servants sitting down to tea with family members in the main house.

"We were supposed to meet here like we usually do," Ella said. "I had an issue with my stove, though, so I couldn't make the tea. We ended up in the south garden instead and Mrs. Ballywick made the tea for us. Aunt Hattie never ventured out there. It was too far from the main house."

"Is the south garden that far?" I asked.

"Not for anyone else," Ella replied. "Aunt Hattie tended to stick to the inside of the house is all. The fact that she was outside on her birthday was a big deal."

So Ella could have taken the key to the mead cellar from Sampson and slipped it back later without him realizing it. That meant she had motive, access, and opportunity.

"What did you and Sampson talk about over tea?" I asked.

"The party, of course." Ella appeared thoughtful. "My dating prospects. Sampson is very sweet. He wants to vet any potential suitors."

I smiled to myself. Sampson was a little more fatherly toward Ella than Simon was toward me, probably the result of our different personalities.

"And, as far as you know, Sampson didn't have issues with Hattie?" I asked. "No recent disagreements?"

"Not that I know of," Ella said. "Like I said, Sampson is a sweetheart. I can't imagine him harming anyone." With those words, she lopped the head off a flower with her shears.

"Let me know if you're interested in meeting with Artemis and I can arrange an introduction," I said. *Assuming you're not a murderer.*

"I'll consider it, thanks." She wiped her brow with her sleeve. "Right now, I'd like to focus on maintaining my house and garden until it's time to move into the main house."

I glanced over my shoulder at the charming little house. "What will you do with this place?"

"Rent it out for extra income, I think," she said. "It'll be part of the estate, so I'll have the freedom to do whatever I want with it." She smiled as she looked at the house. "Wow. Freedom to do whatever I want. I never thought I'd be able to say those words." Her expression clouded over. "I don't want to act like I've been some hostage under Aunt Hattie's thumb. It wasn't like that. She never explicitly told me what I could and couldn't do."

I gave her a sympathetic look. "You felt like you couldn't live your life to its fullest, Ella. Whether she explicitly set rules or not, it sounds like she had control over important aspects of your life."

Ella offered a small smile. "Not anymore."

No, not anymore.

CHAPTER THIRTEEN

"I THOUGHT we were going to tea," Aunt Hyacinth said. "This is the road to Haverford House."

"We are going to tea," I said.

My aunt sniffed. "You and Marley seem perfectly capable of visiting Artemis Haverford without any involvement from me."

We rolled down the long driveway of Haverford House. Marley and I had made an appointment with the matchmaker without telling Aunt Hyacinth what we were up to, mostly because we knew she'd reject the idea.

"This isn't a social call," I replied. "We're going for you."

My aunt recoiled. "For me? Whatever do you mean?"

"It's time to set the matchmaking wheels in motion," I said.

My aunt locked the car door. "Don't be absurd. I don't do matchmaking. I'm a Rose."

"Aunt Hyacinth, you should be spending time with someone you care about," Marley said. "Someone you can share your days with."

"I share my days with my family," she said. "I don't need more than that."

"Maybe if you had someone special, you'd be less focused on everyone else's choices," I said.

My aunt fixed me with a thousand yard stare. "You really don't mince words, do you?"

I shrugged. "Life's too short."

She heaved a sigh. "I don't know that Artemis is the right matchmaker for me. She's so…."

"Bourgeois?" Marley interjected.

Aunt Hyacinth gave a firm nod. "Exactly." She tapped the window between the driver and us. "Simon, you can drop us right at the base of the front steps."

"You know about Jefferson, right?" Marley asked.

"Her ghostly manservant?" my aunt asked. "Yes, I'm aware of him and their, ahem, curious relationship."

Phew. That was one awkward thing I wouldn't need to explain. It was hard enough to explain it to myself.

"Mom, did you mention to Aunt Hyacinth about the wand she gave me?"

My aunt's head jerked to attention. "What about the wand? It's a family heirloom, not some thrift store purchase."

I laughed. "I know it's an heirloom. I also know that it's filled with more energy than I could handle. Marley and I were wondering about the wand's history."

Aunt Hyacinth gazed out the window. "A story for another time, perhaps."

"You gave Marley the wand, but you don't want to share its history?" I asked.

"I don't know *all* its history," Aunt Hyacinth said. She arched a sculpted eyebrow at me. "You picked up on its energy during psychometry?"

"Marigold blabbed, didn't she?" I asked.

"Marigold didn't blab, as she's not a child," my aunt replied. "She felt the experience was worth mentioning, as do you, apparently."

"Don't you have the same set of psychic skills that I do?" I asked. I knew my mother was particularly strong in that area, not that anyone gave my maternal side credit. It was all about the Roses in Starry Hollow.

"Not quite," my aunt said begrudgingly. I could hear the dissatisfaction in her tone. Then again, dissatisfied seemed to be her normal state of mind.

Simon pulled the car in front of Haverford House and came around to open the door for Aunt Hyacinth. Marley and I made it to the front door first and it popped open before we had a chance to knock.

"Hi, Jefferson." Marley breezed straight in. Her home away from home. Come to think of it, she had several of those. Lucky girl. A far cry from our shoebox apartment and no close friends or relatives to visit.

I felt the chill of the ghostly manservant's presence as I entered the foyer. Clementine trotted over to greet us, her mangy tail high and proud. Marley crouched down to give her a proper hello.

Aunt Hyacinth stepped into the foyer behind us and surveyed the space with a pinched expression.

"Everything good?" I asked in a quiet voice.

"I thought she had servants," Aunt Hyacinth said. She didn't bother to lower her voice.

"She has Jefferson," I said.

"Right," my aunt replied, in a tone that suggested we'd be discussing this disaster on the car ride home.

A cold breeze tugged us toward the parlor room. Marley walked ahead with Clementine in her arms, chatting to Jefferson about her birthday.

"That child makes friends wherever she goes," my aunt said. The note of pride in her voice stirred something deep in my heart.

Artemis Haverford sat in her chair, awaiting our arrival. She'd clearly taken great pains with her appearance, likely because of Aunt Hyacinth's presence today. She wore a pale yellow dress with tiny embroidered flowers, and her white hair was loose and adorned with a sprig of yellow flowers. A tray of tea and all the accouterments were already on the table.

"I hope you don't take it as a sign of disrespect if I don't get up," Artemis said apologetically. "These old bones have their own way of doing things."

"Of course we don't," I said. When I leaned down to greet her with a kiss on the cheek, the smell of lavender filled my nostrils.

"Nice to see you, Artemis," my aunt said, with a slight nod.

"And you," Artemis replied. "Whatever anti-aging spell you're using, do keep it up. It's working wonders."

"You're too kind," Aunt Hyacinth said.

Marley flung her arms around the witch's neck and planted a sloppy kiss on her wrinkled cheek. "I've missed you."

"Same here. I might have a little something for you, birthday girl," Artemis said, smiling. "Please sit, everyone. Jefferson will pour the tea."

Aunt Hyacinth observed with mild interest as an invisible hand set to work on the teacups. "There's nothing like good help, is there? I don't know where I'd be without Simon and Mrs. Babcock. They are truly gifts from the gods."

It occurred to me how grateful my aunt genuinely was for the work provided by her employees. And they knew it, too. A marked difference from Hattie.

Artemis cast a sly smile in Jefferson's direction. "I don't know how I'd live without Jefferson. As absurd as it sounds given that he's incorporeal, he's my rock."

I knew their relationship was...unconventional, but I thought it was wonderful that they had each other. I felt a slight rush of air as Jefferson leaned past me to—I imagine—kiss Artemis on the cheek. Not quite the same relationship that Simon had with my aunt. Theirs was far more professional.

I settled on the settee with my aunt, while Marley sat cross-legged on the floor with Clementine. Thankfully, no one seemed bothered that she wasn't following the 'young lady' rules by sitting quietly with her ankles crossed in the chair.

"Jefferson, if you could bring out Marley's present now, before we get started, that would be best," Artemis said.

We sipped our tea and made polite conversation while Jefferson left to retrieve the birthday gift.

"I hear that your venerable editor-in-chief is back on the market," Artemis said to my aunt.

My antennae shot up. Interestingly, I noticed that Marley kept her attention on the cat. It seemed to me that this news would be of great interest to her.

"Is that so?" Aunt Hyacinth asked. "What happened with the nymph? Sally? Molly?" She looked around helplessly.

"Holly," Marley said.

"Yes, that's it. I knew it was a common name," my aunt said.

I bit back a smile. Leave it to my aunt to use someone's name as a passive-aggressive insult.

"Are you certain?" Aunt Hyacinth asked. "He hasn't mentioned anything to me and he joined us for dinner recently."

"Without Holly," Marley said pointedly.

Artemis took another sip of tea and set her cup back on the saucer. "I have it on good authority that Holly was seen rampaging her way through a shop after blowing off steam at her beau." Artemis tapped the ends of her fingernails together. "Ladies don't behave that way in a happy, healthy relationship. If they haven't ended things yet, I daresay the moment is upon us."

I sat in silence, absorbing the information. I figured from the outset that it wouldn't last, but the reality of its relatively quick demise was throwing me for a loop.

"I'm surprised to hear about her unladylike behavior," my aunt said. "If nothing else, I found her almost too ladylike. Girlish even. Not at all the type of woman I expected a vampire like Alec to be drawn to."

"I'm not surprised," Marley said. "Holly was a distraction and now I guess he's ready to get back on track."

"On track?" my aunt repeated. "On track for what?"

Marley stroked the cat's back. "Whoever he's meant to be with. I'm pretty sure Holly isn't the one."

"As I always say," Artemis said with a not-so-subtle look at me, "no path is ever certain."

I wasn't sure whether she meant that my path with the sheriff wasn't certain or whether Alec's path wasn't certain. Ugh. Don't confuse me, old lady witch with psychic abilities! I'd closed one door so I could walk through another with the sheriff. That was the plan.

A large wrapped box with a bright blue ribbon floated into the room and diverted the conversation away from Alec. Marley's eyes went from almonds to walnuts. "For me?"

Artemis beamed at her. "Who else, my lovely? I made certain not to use any pink wrappings because I know how fond you are of blue. I have to admit, it was a struggle."

"Thank you, Artemis." Marley plucked the box from the air. "And you, too, Jefferson. Can I open it now, Mom?"

"I think that would be acceptable," I said.

Marley carefully untied the ribbon and then opened the present, sliding her finger under the tape so as not to rip the gorgeous paper.

"Marley, dear, what are you doing?" Aunt Hyacinth asked.

"Preserving the paper," Marley said. "I might want to reuse it."

An audible gulp came from my aunt. "My word, Marley, you're a Rose. You don't need to reuse anything."

Marley gave her a blank look. "But it's such pretty paper. I don't want to throw it away."

I nudged my aunt with my leg, hoping she'd let it go. There was no point in arguing over paper.

"I'm glad you like it," Artemis said. "Now I hope you like the gift just as much as the wrapping."

Marley opened the box and I could see the conflicted expression on her face.

"What is it, sweetheart?" I prompted.

"An herb organizer," Marley said. She turned the present toward me so that I could have a better view. It was the ideal gift for someone like Marley, who loved organization as much as she loved animals. There were tiny drawers with blank labels.

Artemis frowned. "I'm sensing I might have missed the mark on this one."

"You haven't at all," I said. "It just shows how well you know Marley."

"I love it," Marley said glumly.

"Her magic hasn't manifested," Aunt Hyacinth said. She wasn't about to beat around the Rose bush. "We're not certain whether it's a glitch or her father's human genes."

Artemis folded her hands in her lap and looked calmly at Marley. "Do you think I am the kind of witch who would give you a gift that you cannot use, my lovely?"

139

Marley blinked back tears. "No, Artemis."

"No, indeed." Artemis held up a finger. "I expect you to use your best handwriting to label those drawers because you *will* be mastering herbology. You'll come to Haverford House if need be. I have a garden full of herbs to assist you."

Marley seemed to perk up. "I would love that. Thank you so much."

I fixed my gaze on Artemis. "You're sure? You've seen a vision in the cobwebs or whatever weird thing you do?"

Artemis suppressed a smile. "I haven't consulted the runes or the cards, but I have a sixth sense about such matters, and I'd bet good coin that Marley has the Rose genes."

"A wonderful gift," my aunt said. "You've been too kind to my family, Artemis."

"On the contrary, they've been too kind to me," Artemis replied firmly. "I was nothing but the elderly matchmaker in town before these two arrived. They reminded me what it's like to have friends rather than clients."

My aunt laughed. "Well, that seems rather at odds with the purpose of our visit today."

"Not at all," Artemis said. "I'm thrilled to work with you, Hyacinth. Anything that gives me a reason to see these two is a huge plus in my book."

Aunt Hyacinth flicked a stray hair away from her eye and wore her best 'get-down-to-business' expression. "Now, how does this work exactly? We discuss eligible gentlemen in the area? I provide a list of possibilities?"

"If you have a list of possibilities, then I don't see why I'd be of use to you," Artemis said.

"Fair point," my aunt replied.

"I can work with any number of tools," Artemis said. "Cards, runes, dice, meditation, numerology. Whatever you're comfortable with. First, though, I'd like to assess your energy." Artemis leaned forward and held out her hands in a way that reminded me of Rhys Meridien.

Aunt Hyacinth gave me a curious look before reaching out to join their fingertips. Artemis closed her eyes and began drawing slow, deep breaths. Everyone was silent to the point where I worried Artemis had fallen into a post-tea coma, but, after a couple of tense minutes, her eyes popped open and she began to speak.

"Your energy is very powerful," Artemis said.

Well, duh. The old witch had to do better than that or my aunt was going to walk.

"Of course it is," my aunt began, but Artemis shushed her.

"Please, no distractions," the elderly witch said. "I need to process."

Aunt Hyacinth's mouth formed a thin line of displeasure. She didn't like to be shushed by anyone.

"I sense a blockage," Artemis said.

My aunt's eyebrows knitted together. "A clogged artery? Should I see the healer?"

"Not your physical health," Artemis said. "Your spiritual energy. The blockage makes it difficult for you to connect with potential mates."

My aunt flinched at the word 'mate.' Marley didn't miss it either because she said, "Why does that word bother you, Aunt Hyacinth?"

My aunt flashed an innocent look. "Which word?"

"Mate," Marley said, undeterred. My aunt would have to work harder to get out from under Marley's firm thumb. "You're at a matchmaker's. Finding a mate is sort of the point."

"Mate is such a...primitive word," my aunt replied primly. "I'm a descendant of the One True Witch, not a garden-variety shifter. I prefer a term like partner."

"Duly noted," Artemis said.

Talk about blockage. My aunt couldn't open her mind to the possibility of a partner because she was too busy being close-minded about anyone and everyone outside the Rose family. It was a miracle she'd married the first time.

"I do sense that you are content with your situation, which is nice," Artemis said. "You don't project longing the way many women do."

My aunt seemed pleased with this description. She didn't want to be like 'other women.'

"By the same token," Artemis continued, "there is an emptiness that seems like it could be filled by a...partner. A romantic partnership keeps you not just living, but alive."

"I've been thinking about that murdered morgen," my aunt said. "I don't want to become a bitter prune with so many enemies at my death that no one can guess which one killed me." It was a rare and vulnerable admission for my formidable aunt and I was proud of her for having the courage to make that statement. No one wanted to die amongst enemies disguised as loved ones. What an awful way to go. My aunt was right, though—her own behavior was a determining factor. She had the power to improve the situation and, if a romantic partner was going to help smooth her rough edges, then I was all in favor.

"Aunt Hyacinth, you've already shown that you're different from Hattie," Marley said.

My aunt regarded Marley with interest. "How so?"

"You haven't freaked out on me for not having magic," Marley said. "In fact, you've been really patient and seem to think it still might work out."

Artemis released my aunt's hands. "The child makes an excellent point. You might not be as rigid as you believe."

"Oh, she's rigid," I interjected. "It's just that she's not as bad as Hattie was, and we have time to make sure she doesn't stumble onto Bitter Highway as the years pass."

Aunt Hyacinth frowned. "Why, thank you, Ember."

I offered a big smile. "I do my part."

My aunt decided on cards for the matchmaking part of her reading, so Jefferson cleared away the tea tray to make room. I expected tarot cards, but was surprised to see a pack of Uno cards from the human world.

"We can find Aunt Hyacinth a boyfriend and then play a round of Uno," I joked.

Marley brightened. "I love this game."

Artemis seemed confused. "These are not for games. They're for readings." She shuffled the deck and then cut it in half before sliding one section closer to my aunt and fanning them out. "Choose three cards."

My aunt withdrew three of the cards and held them close to her chest. "Do I reveal them?"

Artemis's eyes sparkled. "If you expect me to read them, then yes."

My aunt placed them on the coffee table for all to see—a Draw Four, a red eight, and a Wild.

"Two of those look good, I guess," Marley said.

"I don't want good," my aunt sniffed. "I want the best."

"But what is the best?" Artemis asked. "We're talking about romantic partners specific to you. 'The best' will be different for you than it is for Ember, for example."

"True," my aunt said. "There's no accounting for taste."

"Is that a dig at Granger?" I asked. "Because that's more than a little rude considering I'm sitting here with you right now."

"Granger is your Holly," my aunt said. "Nothing more than a distraction. An attractive nuisance, if you like."

My whole body tensed. "Granger is nothing like Holly."

Artemis held up a hand. "All this negative energy will disrupt the reading."

I clamped my mouth closed for the sake of Artemis. Even Marley looked mildly unsettled and I knew she was still rooting for Alec.

"I only mean that my preference is still that you settle down with a nice wizard like Aster has," my aunt said. "There's still time."

"Let's focus on you, okay?" I said.

Artemis tapped the card with the red eight. "This is a gentleman who comes from humble beginnings, but has set himself apart, whether through business or magic or some other means, I can't be sure."

"An achiever," my aunt said with a pleased nod. "I like that."

Artemis moved to the Draw Four. "Hmm. Not an ideal choice, but very seductive and charming. He may seem like what you want, but ultimately he will leave you feeling alone."

"I guess the Wild card speaks for itself," I said.

"It does," Artemis agreed. "He's going to take you by surprise and offer you a ride worth taking. Bumpy and uncomfortable at times, but exhilarating."

"And how do I meet these gentlemen?" my aunt asked. "And, more importantly, how will I know which is which?"

Artemis laughed gently. "I can pinpoint the men, but your next question…That's the tricky part. Only you can decide which is which."

"So what's next?" I asked.

"When she's ready," Artemis said. She glanced at my aunt. "And I'm not sure that she is, but when the time comes, she can find the first prospective match at Balefire Beach."

My aunt burst into laughter. "The beach? Surely, you're joking."

"The cards don't lie, Hyacinth," Artemis said.

"I love the beach," Marley said. "I'll go with you anytime."

Aunt Hyacinth exhaled. "Fine. What happens? I show up and scan the sand for my prince?"

"You be you, Hyacinth Rose-Muldoon," Artemis said. She swept up the cards and reshuffled the deck. "And the rest will fall into place."

CHAPTER FOURTEEN

IT DIDN'T TAKE LONG for Marley to convince my aunt to accompany us to Balefire Beach. Marley was desperate to use her bodyboard from the Wish Market for the hundredth time and I wanted to keep her mind off the magic that still wasn't manifesting.

We barely settled into our beach chairs when Marley took off with her board, kicking up sand in Aunt Hyacinth's direction. You would've thought my aunt had just been molested by a swarm of locusts the way she whipped out her wand and eviscerated the tiny grains of sand.

"You're dangerous at the beach," I said. I reached for Alec's book that Marley had tossed into the beach bag. I figured I'd start reading it while she was otherwise engaged. As long as I was careful not to knock her bookmark out of place, I considered myself safe.

"I'm dangerous everywhere, darling," my aunt replied. She tucked her wand into the pouch of her beach bag and adjusted her sunhat. I'd assumed her elegant style would seem out of place on the beach, but my aunt managed to have a chic beachwear look that made me rethink my own tankini and white mesh cover-up. Even her hair was carefully styled under the wide-brimmed hat.

Is this sun lounger taken? My familiar climbed onto Marley's empty chair and made himself at home.

"Raoul, what are you doing here?"

What? Raccoons can't like the beach? I love it here. One of my favorite places to contemplate the state of the universe.

As I rolled my eyes, I noticed that my aunt was doing the same. Of course, she was responding to his mere presence rather than what he'd said.

"We're scouting for my aunt's new boyfriend," I said.

My aunt silenced me with a look. "We're not sharing this information, Ember."

"He can read my mind," I said. "It's not something I'd expend the energy to shield from him."

No, you save that for your nightly Kegel exercises and your fantasies about....

I glared at him. "That's enough out of you, dumpster diva."

Aunt Hyacinth adjusted her seaside kaftan covered in images of starfish. "Where is this prospective match? I'm uncomfortably hot already."

Tell her that's menopause, not the sun, Raoul said.

I'll let you do the honors, I said. *I happen to value my life.* I read a few pages of the book, occasionally glancing up to watch Marley ride the waves and make sure she didn't get sucked out to sea by the current or some mischievous mermaid.

"Ember, how lovely to see you." I glanced up to see Avonne, looking ridiculously beautiful in a one-piece golden swimsuit and oversized sunglasses.

"Hi, Avonne," I said. "This is my aunt, Hyacinth, and my familiar, Raoul."

Va-va-voom, Raoul said. One of the many times I was grateful to be the only one who could hear him.

"Hyacinth, such an honor to meet you in person," Avonne said. "I serve with your daughter, Aster, on a few boards."

"Yes, she's mentioned you," my aunt said. "Are you here with your family?" My aunt scanned the beach.

"Yes, they're right over there setting up." Avonne pointed to where Stone was spreading out a blanket while two children pulled toys from a bucket.

"What a gorgeous family," my aunt said. She gave me a knowing look. "See, Ember. That's what you should aspire to."

Inwardly, I groaned. "I have a family. In fact, I'm here with them right now."

Damn straight, Raoul said, folding his paws in his lap.

"The kids are ecstatic that their father is finally joining us," Avonne said. "He's been so busy lately that we've barely seen him for meals, let alone family time."

I watched as Stone lifted one of the children onto his shoulders. The child squealed with delight.

"Sounds familiar," my aunt murmured, and I knew she was reminded of Aster and Sterling. Of course, she had no idea about Sterling's indiscretion and I had no intention of telling anyone. Sterling had put the whole incident to rest and was determined to be the best husband and father he could be.

"He's been making more of an effort since Grandmother died," Avonne said, smiling over her shoulder. "He knows what a shock it was."

"I was so sorry to hear about her passing," Aunt Hyacinth said.

"Thank you. I was disappointed to hear the sheriff say that the investigation has stalled a bit," Avonne said. "I hate feeling like things are out of joint."

"I totally feel you," I said. I caught sight of Marley as she managed to stay atop the board despite a massive wave. I breathed a sigh of relief. "I'm sure there'll be a break soon. There always is."

Stone walked over, each hand dragging a child behind him. Their half-hearted protests were full of giggles. "I found these two raiding our treasure box, Avonne. What do we do with them? Have them walk the plank?"

Hose 'em down first before they smell, Raoul said.

Not your kind of treasure, I replied.

"Dunk them in the water and see if they'll reveal their evil plans," Avonne said.

The children screeched.

"Marley wouldn't mind a couple of playmates out there," I said.

"Marley?" Stone repeated. He shot a quick look at the water where Marley had just glided back onto shore. "She looks familiar. Does she have an after-school job at one of the shops in town?"

"If coming straight home and doing all her homework without being asked qualifies as an after-school job, then yes," I replied.

Stone grinned at his wife. "Speaking of jobs, I may need a sexy dunking assistant. Any applicants?"

Avonne flipped her sunglasses to the top of her head. "Consider the position filled."

"Have fun," I called.

Some guys have all the luck, Raoul grumbled.

"We're here for Aunt Hyacinth, not for you," I said.

A shadow dropped over us. "You are the last trio I would expect to find hanging out here."

I shaded my eyes and dared to look up into the cheeky grin of Wyatt Nash. "How's it going, Wyatt?"

"I thought I felt a cold wind blow in," my aunt said.

"That's just your breath," Wyatt shot back.

"Not here with your children, I take it," my aunt said. "I'm sure that would cramp your style."

"Actually, I'm here with Linnea and the kids," Wyatt said. "We decided to spend a little family time together."

"Let me guess," my aunt said. "Linnea arranged the excursion and you tagged along."

"That's about the size of it," Linnea said, appearing beside him. "Mother, I have to admit that I'm more than a little surprised to see you here."

"She's searching for suitors," I said. Aunt Hyacinth gave me a look that would have reduced a lesser witch to tears, but I held firm.

"What a coincidence," Wyatt said. "I'm keeping my eye open for that sweet thing from Rainbow's End. Newly single nymphs are like umbrellas on a cloudy day—they're always a good bet."

It took my brain a minute to process. "Are you talking about Holly?"

"Your boss's girlfriend," Wyatt said. "I guess ex-girlfriend. Don't know her name." He didn't seem interested in learning it either. Typical Wyatt.

"Are you sure they've broken up?" I asked. "I know there've been a few incidents, but I don't think it's clear."

"You seem rather convinced that they're still together, despite everyone's evidence to the contrary," my aunt said.

"It's pretty clear," Wyatt replied. "My buddy overheard them in the Wish Market. She was shrieking at him like a banshee on steroids. They are one hundred percent finito."

"I thought it was an argument and that they'd work it out," I said.

"Apparently not," Wyatt said with a shrug. "Not every relationship is worth saving." He winked at Linnea. "Present company excepted, of course."

Linnea glared at him. "If we were worth saving, we'd still be together."

"Come on, honey. Admit it. You miss me." Wyatt puckered his lips.

Linnea pushed a hand against his mouth. "Only when I need something fixed at Palmetto House and my magic isn't getting the job done."

"Oh, I always get the job done," Wyatt said. "You must remember that much about me."

Linnea grew flustered. "Take your bravado elsewhere, please."

"I'm trying," Wyatt said. "But she's not here."

Linnea sighed in exasperation. "Join your offspring in the water while I chat with my family. Playtime is what you're good at, after all."

I was pleased that Bryn and Hudson were here to hang out with Marley in the water. She'd want to stay until sunset even if she were alone. Better to have company.

"So are you really here to check out the men?" Linnea asked, pulling up a chair.

Aunt Hyacinth harrumphed. "I am here under the advice of a matchmaker, but I must say that I'm beginning to doubt her abilities. This all feels like a waste of time."

"Quality time with your family is never a waste of time," I said. "It's gone in the blink of an eye."

My aunt lowered her gaze. "I suppose that's true. My husband and I were very good about quality time."

"You were," Linnea said. She patted her mother's hand. "And now your children have children of their own and busy lives. It's time for you to devote attention to someone else. Someone who cares for you and makes you laugh."

It was difficult to picture Aunt Hyacinth carefree and laughing. The image did not compute.

"I've been so busy trying to arrange matches for you and

Florian that I've neglected myself," my aunt admitted. "And since I've failed spectacularly anyway, maybe it's best that I redirect my efforts."

"I think that's a fine idea," Linnea said. "I'm glad you went to see a matchmaker."

"Grandmother, come in the water," Bryn called, waving wildly from the surf.

My aunt's brow lifted. "In the water? Has she gone feral?"

"Mother," Linnea said. "Your teen granddaughter still likes you enough to want to be seen with you at the beach. Do you know what a rare gift that is?"

"I'll go as far as the water's edge," she said. "No further."

"That's right," I said. "Live on the edge, Aunt Hyacinth."

She slid off her sandals first. Then she stood and smoothed the front of her kaftan before sauntering down to see her grandchildren.

"This is unbelievable," Linnea said. "Has someone put a potion in her cocktail?"

"I think she wants to turn over a new leaf," I said. "Hattie's death has been a wake up call for her, I think."

"Good," Linnea said. "Whatever it takes." She noticed the book on my lap. "Alec's latest book?"

My cheeks reddened. "A gift to Marley. I was browsing it while she was in the water."

"I see." Linnea didn't elaborate. I knew she was partial to Granger, not only because he was her former brother-in-law, but because she genuinely cared about him.

Your aunt is going to go candle over wick out there if she's not careful, Raoul said.

I glanced up to see Aunt Hyacinth wading further out into the water than I expected. The bottom of her kaftan was soaking wet, but she didn't seem to care. She was focused on Marley's demonstration of how to ride the board. It was then that I saw the huge wave rolling toward them.

My mouth opened, but there wasn't enough time to warn them. The wave crashed over the group, scattering them like pieces on a game board. Marley popped up instantly and my heart relaxed. I counted all the heads except one.

"Where's Mother?" Linnea was on her feet before I could say a word.

"There she is," I said, pointing in the distance to the white-blond head bobbing up and down. The current had managed to pull her further out to sea. "Is she a strong swimmer?"

"She's Mother," Linnea said. "She's a strong everything."

"She was taken by surprise," I said. "I'm sure she needs help." Even the best swimmers could be outmatched by the sea.

I'd only taken a few steps toward the shore when I realized that Aunt Hyacinth's form was getting closer and closer. Then I noticed the powerful arms lifting her clear of the water.

"Is that a…?" I squinted.

"A merman," Linnea said. "Sweet Goddess of the Moon. Look at those arms."

He emerged from the water, still holding my aunt's drenched body. Although she appeared conscious, she seemed to be in shock. His fin dissolved into legs as the air reached them and he walked onto the sand, lowering my aunt to the ground and deftly administering CPR. I didn't even know if it was medically necessary, but my aunt didn't seem to mind.

Linnea and I ran over to join the crowd that now surrounded them. I immediately noticed the merman's bare muscular chest and thick salt and pepper hair.

"No need to make a fuss," my aunt said. "I'm perfectly fine, thank you." She sat up, dusting the sand from her outfit. With the wet kaftan clinging to her body, it quickly became apparent that my aunt kept her hourglass figure under wraps thanks to her penchant for oversized dresses.

The merman examined her. "Are you certain? I saw you ingest quite a bit of water before I was able to get to you."

My aunt coughed. "I'll be fine. I'll go at once to see the healer."

"At least allow me to accompany you," he said. "Tell him what I witnessed."

"If you insist," my aunt said. I thought she'd relented far too easily. "I'm Hyacinth Rose-Muldoon." She tucked a soggy stand of hair behind her ear.

"Zale Murphy," he said, and shook her hand. "Can you walk? I'm happy to carry you. You're light as a pelican's feather."

"I can stand on my own two feet," she said firmly.

He didn't bother to disguise a smile. "Very well then."

"Marley and I will find a ride back," I said. "Don't worry about us."

"I wasn't," Aunt Hyacinth called over her shoulder.

Raoul snickered. *I guess she found her prospective match.*

"Yes, but which one is he?" I mused. Was the merman a red eight, a Draw Four, or the Wild card? Only time would tell.

CHAPTER FIFTEEN

THE SHERIFF and I sat in the Whitethorn, enjoying the last of our dessert and drinks. We'd discussed Hattie's murder at length and seemed no closer to figuring out which suspect was responsible. They all seemed to have motive, access, and opportunity.

The sheriff gazed at me over his pint of ale. "I like coming here with you, even if we talk about murder. I've been coming here so long on my own, I forgot how nice company can be."

"I'm sure you could've had company any time you wanted it," I said. "That star on your shirt attracts all kinds." There was no shortage of women in Starry Hollow eager to provide the sexy sheriff with an evening of companionship.

He glanced down at his shirt. "Oh, so it's the star, is it? Not my rugged good looks or my charming personality?"

I waved my hand in front of him. "It's the whole package. Even the earnest expression you wear so well. Women think they love a bad boy, but they want you more."

His brow lifted. "They want me, do they? Can't say I've seen evidence of that, Rose."

"Only because you haven't been paying attention. It's called willful oblivion."

"Or maybe because I only have eyes for one lady in particular and she happens to be seated across from me right now."

"You don't have to flatter me to get invited to my sleep-over party. I told you it's on the horizon."

He leaned closer. "How close is this horizon, would you say?"

"Sorry to interrupt," a perky voice said.

"Holly," I said, unable to hide my surprise. Instinctively, I looked behind her for any sign of Alec. Maybe I'd finally get confirmation that the rumors were true.

"Alec is in the men's room," Holly said, as though reading my thoughts. So much for everyone's so-called 'evidence.'

I laughed. "That vampire has the bladder of an eight months' pregnant woman." I didn't know whether to ask about the status of their relationship. It seemed intrusive.

"I don't mean to interrupt your date," Holly said. "You two are just the cutest together, by the way. Makes me want to fall in love all over again." She sighed dramatically.

"You do it right the first time and you get to feel that way every day," the sheriff said. He quickly realized how his comment sounded. "Sorry, Holly. I didn't mean to suggest that you chose poorly."

"Oh, I know." Holly cast a concerned glance over her shoulder, but Alec was still nowhere in sight. Maybe he was hiding because he'd spotted the sheriff and me. It was hard to tell with the emotionally impenetrable vampire.

"Would you like to join us for a drink?" the sheriff asked. I nearly kicked him under the table. The last thing I wanted to do was watch Holly and Alec together. If they were in their making up phase, it would be too brutal to witness.

"No, but thanks," Holly replied. "Alec and I need some

alone time. I only wanted to say thank you to Ember for raising such a wonderful daughter. I meant to tell you when I saw you in the coffee shop, but I was a little distracted at the time. It's hard enough to raise a good one when both parents are in the picture, but you've managed to do this on your own." She gave my shoulder a gentle pat. "I don't know what your secret is, but keep it up."

"No secret," I said. "I take no credit for the marvel that is Marley. She's her own person."

"Well, either way, it was above and beyond of her to bake that burstberry pie. I know Alec's not a fan, but it's always been one of my favorites. It took a little time, but I made my way through the whole thing and finally finished two days ago." She placed a hand flat on her stomach. "I have the extra pounds to prove it."

I froze. "My daughter baked a pie? Marley?"

Holly laughed lightly. "Do you have another one?"

My head went fuzzy. "When did Marley bring you a pie?"

"She stopped by after school about a week or so ago," Holly said. "She seemed very proud of herself, but she told me some of her stumbling blocks, so I showed her a few baking tricks to help her the next time around."

"Thanks," I said slowly. "That was kind of you."

"Oh, there's Alec," Holly said. "I'll see you around."

"Enjoy yourselves," I said.

Holly intercepted him before he could make his way over. Despite the fact that they were out alone together, their body language seemed distant. To be fair, Alec's always seemed distant, but Holly had a tendency to drape herself all over him. I tore my gaze away.

"Something's not right with them," the sheriff said.

"In so many ways." I continued to sit there staring at my drink, while my mind reeled. Marley brought her a pie? On the one hand, Holly was right—it was incredibly thoughtful.

On the other hand, I felt...betrayed. It was ridiculous, of course. Marley didn't do anything wrong. I had no desire for her to dislike Holly, and Marley was still Alec's biggest fan. I hated that I even had these feelings, especially when the sheriff was right here in front of me being his wonderfully open and adoring self. Great balls of complex emotions, Rhys Meridien was right. I needed help.

"That was sweet of Marley to bake a pie," the sheriff said.

"Sounds like she did a good job, too," I said. "Better than I would've done." We all knew I didn't exactly excel in the culinary arts. If I used the microwave without anything catching fire, that was a win.

"You seem bothered," the sheriff said. "Any particular reason?"

Damn the sheriff and his investigative nose. "I'm just trying to figure out how my daughter would manage to bake a pie and bring it over to Holly's without me knowing." And why she wouldn't think to mention such a nice gesture. Because she worried that it would upset me? "I'll have to ask her about it in the morning when I see her." She'd likely be asleep by the time I got home tonight.

The sheriff swallowed the last of his ale. "If you're sure that's all that's bothering you."

It was all that I was willing to admit. The sheriff deserved better than to be caught in the net of my emotional Ping-Pong. "Thank you for putting up with me. I know I'm not easy."

The sheriff glanced up in surprise. "Put up with you? Rose, there's no such thing." He reached across the table to take my hand. "If it weren't for you, I'd be sitting here with Deputy Bolan and his husband right now. Trust me, it's not the same experience."

My mood instantly lightened. Sheriff Nash always

seemed to have a way of coaxing me out of whatever funk I'd created. "I'm lucky to have you, Granger. I mean that."

He squeezed my hand before releasing it. "I think we both know it's the other way around, but I'll take the compliment." He raised his finger to signal for another drink. "Too bad Hattie didn't have anyone special in her life. Could've prevented all that resentment and ill will."

"And her murder," I added. "Let's not forget that minor detail." I took a generous sip of my cocktail.

"If anyone ever offed me, I'd want the motives and opportunities to be so few that it'd be obvious who the culprit is," the sheriff said. "Make Bolan's job easier anyway."

"I think Aunt Hyacinth has taken Hattie's murder to heart," I said. "She seems intent on changing her life."

"Hattie's storm cleared the path for someone else," the sheriff said. "There's a certain poetry to it, I think."

Out of the corner of my eye, I caught sight of Alec and Holly, deep in conversation. For a brief moment, the vampire's gaze flitted to me. If I didn't know they were in a relationship, I would have thought they were conducting a business meeting. It seemed a far cry from all the yelling and stomping she'd apparently been doing.

Part of me struggled with this change in circumstances. Maybe Marley was right—maybe I was afraid of making a 'wrong' choice. I shrugged off the thoughts. No. I'd vowed to walk through the door that Granger had opened and leave Alec behind and I planned to stick to it. I deserved better than what Alec had offered me, which was nothing more than furtive kisses and longing glances. That wasn't a relationship.

The server brought the sheriff another ale. "You plan to nurse that drink all night, Miss Rose?" the server asked. She gave me a friendly wink.

"I think I am," I admitted. "I've got a busy day tomorrow and I don't want to be dragging."

The server nodded and moved on to her other table.

"That sounds awfully responsible, Rose," the sheriff said. "Are you feeling okay?"

"I'm planning to go to the library," I said. "I've asked Delphine to help me find books on magic manifestation."

He gave me a knowing look. "And reasons why it doesn't, I guess."

"The therapist is a good start," I said, "but if there's anything else I should be doing, I want to do it. This is the most important thing in the world to her...."

"I think you're mistaken on that," he said. "*You're* the most important thing to her in the world."

"Well, okay, but you know what I mean."

He tapped the side of his pint glass. "And what if there's nothing to be done? What if she does take after her father? At what point do you stop trying so that she doesn't feel bad about herself?"

"Believe me, Granger, I don't mind either way," I said. "It's Marley who wants this and, as her mom, I want it for her."

"Tough job, being a mom," he said. "Wanting everything to be perfect for your kid."

"I don't want everything to be perfect," I argued. "I only want her to be the best Marley she can possibly be, and if that Marley is meant to have magic, then, by Elvis, I'm going to do everything in my power to make it happen."

His mouth quirked. "You show those proud broomstick mamas how it's done, Rose. Holly's right—you're doing a remarkable job."

My thoughts turned to Holly and the burstberry pie and, suddenly, I wasn't so sure.

. . .

I woke up the next morning, ready to get to the bottom of the burstberry pie mystery. I even made waffles to sweeten her before I began my interrogation.

Marley appeared in the kitchen doorway, rubbing the sleep from her eyes. "I smelled waffles."

PP3 trotted in behind Marley. He took his place under the table and awaited for the inevitable scraps to fall. His version of pennies from Heaven.

Marley poured herself a glass of milk and sat at the table. "My birthday's passed. Why are you making waffles?"

"Can't a mother decide to make waffles for her amazing daughter?" I set a plate and the bottle of syrup in front of Marley.

Marley peered at me. "What's going on? Is this because you feel guilty about my magic?"

I brought my own plate to the table and joined her. "I thought we'd enjoy a chat over a nice, leisurely breakfast."

Marley slowly lowered her fork to the plate. "What's up?"

"I'd like to talk about the burstberry pie," I said.

Marley's guilty expression said it all. She wouldn't last two seconds under the sheriff's scrutiny or Deputy Bolan's well-perfected scowl for that matter.

"What burstberry pie?" she asked. An ineffective stab at innocence.

"The one you made for Holly and Alec, except you already knew that Alec didn't like burstberry pie, so you knew he wouldn't eat any."

Marley fiddled with her fork. "I was trying to do something nice."

I folded my arms. "Nice is not how I would describe what you've done."

Her gaze met mine. "Not nice for her, Mom. For you."

The expression on her face was so sweet and sincere that

my ovaries nearly exploded. "Marley Rose, I would never, ever want you to harm anyone for my sake."

"I didn't hurt her," Marley said. "She's fine."

"Her relationship with Alec is imploding. Everyone in town is talking about her behavior."

Marley lowered her gaze back to the waffles. "People gossip here all the time."

I took her hand. "Marley, listen to yourself. You're better than this. Much better. Besides, you know that I've decided to give my relationship with the sheriff a real chance."

"But I thought that was only because of Holly," Marley said. "That if I got rid of her, you'd change your mind and try to make things work with Alec."

She wasn't *completely* wrong. I had considered it. "Alec doesn't know what he wants, sweetheart, and I would never want to be someone's second choice. If Alec decided to pursue a relationship with Holly for whatever reason, then I accept that."

"What about Sheriff Nash?" Marley asked. "He's *your* second choice. That's unfair to him."

Ooh, snap. Marley wasn't taking any prisoners in this conversation. "Granger has entered this relationship with his eyes wide open and that's his decision." She didn't need to know any more than that. "Now tell me what you did to the burstberry pie."

"I went to a potions shop that some of the kids at school go to sometimes because he sells to non-magical minors," she said. "Devil's Claw. I bought a pre-made potion."

"When did you manage all this?" I asked. And where had I been?

"It was the day before I stayed home sick from school," she said.

"No wonder you felt sick that day," I replied. "Now I understand. What did the potion do?"

162

Marley used her fork to swirl the syrup around on her plate. "You can probably guess. Got Holly fired up over the littlest things. The potion is called Knee-Jerk. A friend at school used it on her mom's boyfriend to prove what a jerk he was."

"But that doesn't prove anything," I said. "It was the potion."

Marley shrugged. "She got rid of her mom's boyfriend, so she got the result she wanted."

I slumped in my chair. Marley was only eleven. The teenage years in a paranormal town were going to be harder than I anticipated.

"And you were hoping to get a similar result," I said.

"I knew Alec wouldn't like her anymore if she was angry and unpleasant all the time. He's too even-tempered. Then they'd break up and she'd leave town."

"Well, she hasn't left town," I said. "And I saw them out together last night." Although things definitely didn't appear rosy.

Marley looked disappointed. "I'm sorry."

"Sorry that you used a potion on her? Or sorry that your plan failed?"

She gave me a sheepish look. "Can it be both?"

"You have to confess what you've done to Holly," I said. "Let her patch things up with Alec. If he knows her behavior wasn't really her, I'm sure they'll be fine."

Marley shifted in her chair. "Do I have to confess *why*?"

I glared at her. "You'd better not or you'll be in even worse trouble." I scraped back my chair and stood. "Finish your waffles and we'll get ready to go."

CHAPTER SIXTEEN

LESS THAN AN HOUR LATER, we were on Holly's doorstep. Marley and I barely spoke on the ride over. I didn't have much experience being disappointed in my daughter and I was struggling with my own reaction. It wasn't the type of incident I could discuss with anyone either, not without explaining why Marley would go to such lengths. It would have to be our secret.

Holly answered the door, looking bedraggled. She didn't seem embarrassed to have visitors. "Well, this is quite the surprise. Come in. You'll have to excuse the mess. I'm in a bit of a packing frenzy."

"Packing?" I echoed.

We stepped inside the apartment and I noticed the boxes lined against the wall. There was a suitcase placed across the sofa cushions and a pile of clothes draped across the arm of the sofa.

"Starry Hollow is a wonderful town, but my time here is up," Holly said good-naturedly. "My lease was only tempo-rary anyway, and I had to make a decision."

So she and Alec hadn't worked it out. I felt terrible. As

conflicted as I felt about Alec, Holly's kind and genuine nature had won me over.

"That's a shame, Holly," I said. "What about Alec?"

The nymph began folding clothes from the arm of the sofa and placing them inside the suitcase. "We weren't meant to be. It's not a surprise, really."

I nudged Marley forward. "Holly, my daughter has something important to tell you that might change your mind."

Holly smiled at Marley. "You do? What's that, honey?"

Marley struggled to speak. "I…I may have added something to the burstberry pie I gave you."

Holly blinked. "What do you mean? You used the wrong ingredients?"

"Sort of," Marley croaked, and I knew she was about to cry. "I bought a potion and added it to the pie."

Holly still wasn't catching on. "What kind of potion? To make it taste better? You didn't trust your baking skills, huh? I totally understand."

Oh, bless. Holly was adorably naive.

"To make you angry," Marley blurted. "To make you a horrible nymph to be around."

Holly stood perfectly still with a pair of pants in her hand, registering the confession. "Hang on a second. *You* were responsible for my crazy behavior?"

Tears streamed down Marley's cheeks. "I'm so sorry. If I could take it back, I would. I've never done anything like that before, but I was so…." She cut herself off, unwilling to throw me under the bus.

Holly offered a sympathetic smile. "Jealous?" She dropped the pants and reached over to stroke Marley's hair. "Listen, honey, I should probably be super upset with you, but I was your age once. I remember what it's like to have a crush on an older guy." Marley opened her mouth to protest, but Holly carried on talking. "His name was Giorgio and he had the most magnificent silver hair." She clasped her hands against her chest. "I was far too young for him, though I didn't realize it at the time. I thought we were written in the stars."

"What happened?" Marley asked. I couldn't tell whether she was playing along or genuinely interested in the outcome.

"He was married, with children younger than me," Holly replied. "I didn't understand that what I felt was just a crush, part of my emotional development." She pinched Marley's cheek. "I forgive you, dear heart, though I should warn you that Alec isn't the right guy for you. He's far too emotionally stunted. Wait for someone with less baggage. I should've known better than to fall for a vampire. When you live that long, you're bound to have issues."

"Is that why you're leaving?" I asked.

Holly nodded, and resumed folding the clothes into neat squares. "I should thank you, Marley. It was a wake-up call, really. I was so caught up in the whirlwind romance, that I didn't stop to see the real Alec."

Tension spread throughout my body. "Who's the *real* Alec?"

Holly placed a pink cardigan twin set in the suitcase. "The one who doesn't communicate his feelings. The one who devotes ninety percent of his time to his work. Even when he wasn't at the office, he was in his home office, writing another book. He's so busy living in the fantasy world of his own design, he's missing out on living in the real world."

"He likes to immerse himself," Marley said. "It shows in his work. You feel like you're there. You smell the exotic spices and picture the stone castles."

Holly rolled up her thong underpants and I averted my gaze. "You view him through spell-tinted glasses and that's fine. You're too young to understand."

I knew that remark would enrage Marley. To her credit, though, she stayed silent.

"Alec can be considerate and generous," I said, feeling defensive on his behalf. It didn't matter that what Holly said was true; I couldn't help myself.

"*Can be* is the key part of that sentence," Holly said. "He *can be* sweet and affectionate and loving, too. Most of the time, though, he's a major downer."

"How's he taking you leaving?" Marley asked.

A truncated breath escaped her. "Who knows? We discussed it at the Whitethorn last night. He was his usual stoic self. He agreed that we probably jumped too quickly." She laughed to herself. "Which is ridiculous. Now that I know him better, I can't understand how this even happened. Alec Hale doesn't jump quickly at anything. He's slow and methodical and thinks everything through a thousand times before he acts."

"Sounds about right," I said.

Holly met my gaze. "I suspect he's had his heart broken. It's made him overly cautious."

"That doesn't explain you," Marley pointed out.

"It does if the heartbreak was recent." Holly returned her focus to the suitcase. "You'd know, wouldn't you, Ember? Maybe you noticed something in the office in the months before he met me?"

I tried to disguise my discomfort. "It's hard to read Alec. If his heart was broken, he certainly didn't share that with me." In fact, he would've taken great pains to hide it.

Holly rolled up a pink dress in a tube and placed it in the suitcase. "I've enjoyed my time here, so it's not a total loss. Like I said, Starry Hollow is a sweet little town. Crazy crime rate for a place this size, though. I don't envy your boyfriend, Ember."

"Will you go back to Rainbow's End?" Marley asked.

"I've been trying to decide. I have a cousin overseas I've been meaning to visit. I may spend a few months with her and then decide what's next. I like an open road."

"So there are no hard feelings between you and Alec?" I asked.

"Not anymore," Holly said. "When I first became angry because of the potion, it got pretty heated, but once we came to our senses, the situation was clear. Like I said, Marley, if it weren't for your potion, it would've taken us much longer to figure out that we weren't compatible."

"I'm sorry it didn't work out," I said. Sort of.

"Alec is a lone wolf," Holly said. "Sorry, I mean a lone vampire." She covered her mouth and giggled. "I can only imagine how he'd react to being called a wolf."

"He's content with his own company," Marley said. "That's not a bad quality."

Holly gave her an indulgent smile. "You really do see the best in him. It's adorable."

"It's been really nice meeting you, Holly," Marley said.

"You've been very gracious about the potion incident," I said. More gracious than I would have been.

Holly closed the lid on her suitcase and zipped the perimeter. "I'm sure you've probably given your daughter an earful, but you seem to be doing something right, so don't beat yourself up over it."

"She's going to be punished for the first time in her life," I said. "That's a pretty big deal in our house."

"For the first time ever? That *is* an accomplishment." Holly tilted her head. "How old are you now?"

"Eleven," Marley replied.

"Oh, that's when your magic manifests, isn't it?" Holly said, completely missing the fact that Marley had not, in fact, come into her magic.

"Yes," Marley said quietly.

"How exciting!" Holly said. She lifted her suitcase off the sofa and placed it on the floor. "I hope it's everything you dreamed it would be. We all deserve to have at least one dream come true, don't we?"

My throat tightened. "Yes, Holly. We absolutely do."

My next order of business was to chew the ear off the owner of Devil's Claw. Selling potions to minors had to be a violation of at least one law, if not more. Marley begged me not to, but I wasn't backing down. Not to excuse her behavior, but she was eleven. This owner was knowingly and regularly selling dangerous potions to minors. There was no excuse for that.

"Where is this place?" I asked.

"Down this side street," Marley replied.

"I can't believe this," I said. "You've only just turned eleven and here we are, traipsing down back alleys to visit illicit potion pushers."

Marley rolled her eyes. "They're not pushers. It's an actual shop." We stopped in front of a dark purple building with white trim. "See?"

Sure enough, the sign outside read—Devil's Claw. "Lead on, Little Miss Mixologist."

Marley hovered outside the door a moment before entering. Her anxiety was palpable. I hated to do this, especially because I'd wanted so desperately for her to assert her independence, but a lesson had to be learned.

A young elf stood behind the counter. His unruly brown hair covered his forehead and the top half of his eyes, but not the tips of his pointy ears. He paled when he noticed me trailing behind Marley.

"Hey, Stuart," Marley greeted him.

"Hey, kid. What's going on?" Stuart tried to act casual, but a bead of sweat had already formed on his forehead.

I examined the rows of herbs and other magical plants. They were prepackaged in jars and other containers, lined up in measurement order. The mixtures were labeled by name and the next line gave a description of the potion's effect. I saw Knee-Jerk there, between Back Talk and Faster, Pussycat.

"Are you the owner of this fine establishment, Stuart?" I asked.

He swallowed hard. "I am."

"I see. And do you make a habit of selling to minors?"

"They're a significant portion of his customer base," Marley interjected. I silenced her with a warning glance. I wanted to hear it from Stuart.

"Are you licensed with the town to conduct this business?" I asked. I had a feeling the answer was no.

The elf scratched the back of his neck. "Licensed?"

Exactly.

"Stuart, you have potentially dangerous substances here." I motioned the bottles nearest to me, full of colorful potions. "Look at these." They were organized by general outcome, simple enough for a minor to understand—anger, sadness, speed.

Speed.

I scanned the labels of the bottles in the row. "Stuart?"

"Yes, Miss Rose?" He sounded panicked.

"This potion here." I touched the bottle labeled Stroke Me. The main ingredient was celeritas. "Have you sold any of these in the past month?"

The elf scratched his chin. "I'd have to check."

I folded my arms. "I'm happy to wait."

He scrambled behind the counter and pulled a ledger from the shelf. He began scanning the pages, starting from today and going backward. Two pages back, he tapped the middle of the page. "Here's one. Same day I sold the potion to your daughter, in fact."

"Do you have a name?" I asked.

"I don't keep that information," Stuart said. "Confidentiality and all that."

"I remember a man here," Marley said. "You waited on me first. He was lingering. I thought it was weird because he seemed to be ready, but he wanted me to go first."

"Did you recognize him?" I asked.

Her eyes grew round. "Yes. I saw him at Balefire Beach the other day. He was with his kids."

My heart seized as the memory came rushing back to me. Stone had told me that Marley looked familiar. He'd even asked if she had a job in town after school. At least that meant he didn't remember seeing her here, which was a relief. If he was capable of killing a two-hundred-year old morgen, who knew what else he was capable of? But what motive could he possibly have? By all accounts, he had money of his own. A happy marriage to Avonne...

Except what if it wasn't? What if, like Sterling and Aster, they'd hit a rough patch and what if Stone had stepped out on his wife? Even worse, what if Hattie had discovered the betrayal and threatened him? That would explain Fern's hostile behavior, as well as Sampson's version of the argument he'd heard between Stone and Hattie. Maybe 'coming clean' hadn't been about a business decision but an affair.

My gut twisted. Stone was the killer, I was sure of it.

"Thanks for your help, Stuart," I said. "Do yourself a favor and take good care of that ledger. I have a feeling you're going to be needing it."

The tips of Stuart's ears turned bright red. "I swear I won't sell to minors anymore. Tell your friends, kid. Devil's Claw is for adults only."

Marley gave him a thumbs up as we left the shop.

"Why are you in such a hurry, Mom?" Marley struggled to keep pace with me on the way back to the car.

"I need to drive over to Granger's," I said. "I have something to tell him."

"Is that man from the beach the one that killed Hattie?" she asked.

I nodded. "And I think I know how and why."

"The sheriff should hire you as his deputy," Marley said.

"Why? So we can get tired of each other and decide we're better off as colleagues? No more relationship plans, Marley."

She huffed. "I only meant because you're good at solving puzzles, and lots of times you do it without magic."

"See?" I said. "Magic isn't necessary to be awesome. It's just an extra, like having freckles or curly hair."

We stopped at the car and continued talking.

"Let's not go overboard," Marley said. "We both know magic is much cooler than having freckles."

I unlocked the car door. "Fine. Magic is cooler, and if I could find a spell to get rid of freckles, I would."

"I'd be okay with not having magic, Mom," Marley said. "Really. I've shown that I don't deserve it anyway. I don't respect its power."

My head whipped toward her. "Marley Rose, don't you dare. You are eleven years old and you are allowed to make mistakes. That doesn't make you a bad person and it doesn't mean you don't deserve the things you want in life. Do you understand me?"

Marley's expression was painfully somber. "I think it will be nice to be like Dad. It's my only connection to him, right? So I get to enjoy life as a human, like he did." She touched the locket around her neck.

What could I say to that? I didn't want to make humanity sound like a bad thing—it wasn't. "Marley, whether you have magic or not, your dad will always be a part of you. You're half Dad, half Mom. That's how biology works. Plain and simple. You're not any less of me just because you don't have magic."

Marley sniffed. "But I want to be just like you," she said softly. "You're my hero."

I moved back to the pavement and pulled her in for a hug. "Where did you come from, perfect child? I think the universe is playing a trick on me and I'm going to wake up and discover you were one long, wonderful dream."

Marley squeezed me hard. "If that's true, then you sleep *a lot* in real life."

I started to laugh, but my laughter was abruptly cut short by a hand clamped over my mouth.

"Don't fight me and I might let your daughter live," the gruff voice said.

Then everything went black.

CHAPTER SEVENTEEN

WHEN I FINALLY CAME TO, the moon was overhead and I was deep in the middle of a forest. My waist was tied to a live oak tree. I wiggled and realized that my ankles were bound together and my hands were tied behind my back. Luckily for me, one weapon was still available to me—my big mouth.

"Marley?" I called. Despite the sliver of moonlight, the forest was too dark to see much of anything.

"Mom?"

Thank sweet baby Elvis. I relaxed slightly, despite our predicament. "Are you hurt?"

"I'm uncomfortable," Marley replied. "Does that count?"

"Your arms and legs are tied?" I asked.

"Yes, and I'm tied to a tree. Can you do any magic to release the ropes?" she asked.

"No, afraid not," a voice said. Stone stepped out of the shadows. "Your mother has a protective spell on her at the moment that prevents her from doing any magic. Another concoction I picked up from Devil's Claw. That place is invaluable." He crouched down and bopped me on the nose with his finger. "No one can hear you scream here either, so don't waste your breath."

"How did you find me so quickly?" I asked.

"I paid that shopkeeper to let me know if anyone came asking about the potion I bought," Stone said. "Good thing I paid him as much as I did or you'd be at the sheriff's office by now."

"I'm sorry, Mom," Marley said. "If I hadn't slowed you down, this never would've happened."

"Aw, aren't kids the greatest?" Stone gave me a mock smile. "That's one of the reasons I have to do this. Preserve my family."

"Is that why you killed Hattie?" I asked. "She found out about your affair?"

He straightened and took a surprised step backward, nearly tripping on a tree root in the process. "How about that? You figured out that part, did you? I thought you'd only unearthed the potion. Now I'm really glad I got my claws in you first."

"Where are we?" I demanded.

"Where does it look like?" he replied. "Nature, sweetie pie. It'll look nice and natural when you're torn to bits by wild animals."

My mind turned to Raoul. If he were within range, maybe he'd sense my distress. The forest was his domain, after all. I had to stall Stone and try to summon Raoul at the same time, unless the protective spell prevented me from communicating with my familiar, too. It was worth a try.

"Let my daughter go," I said. "She isn't part of this."

"Oh, but she is," Stone said. "She knows the truth."

"So does the elf from the shop," I said. "Yet he seems to be walking around, living and breathing."

"Stuart doesn't have a clue," he replied. "Besides, that guy is purely motivated by money, which is something you have plenty of."

"And everyone knows you do, too," I said. "That's one reason no one suspects you."

"The chandelier was a nice touch, too," he said, puffing out his chest. "I rescued Hattie right before the actual murder. Why would I bother saving her life only to turn around and kill her an hour later?" He grinned in the darkness. "Genius, right?"

"I don't know about genius," Marley called. "If it were so genius, my mom and I wouldn't be here right now."

"A smart mouth," Stone said, whirling around. "Do you know what happens to smart mouths in my house?"

I shuddered to think. "I thought your goal was to preserve your family." I wanted his attention back on me, not Marley.

"Of course it is," he said fiercely. "They're *mine*. I'm not letting anyone take them away from me. Hattie would have ruined everything."

"Don't you think you have that a little backward?" I said. "I'm pretty sure it was your affair that would have ruined everything, not Avonne's grandmother knowing about it."

Raoul, can you hear me?

"Avonne isn't going to leave me for someone else," he said. "That morgen is mine. Those kids are mine."

If you can hear me, Marley and I are being held in a forest by Stone Beauregard. Please send help.

"Nothing sexier than a psychotic possessive streak," I said. "And how does your mistress feel about all this? I suppose Fern is yours, too."

He put his face within an inch of mine. "I take what I want and I keep what I want. That's how it works. Understand?"

"I guess that's not how Hattie viewed things," I replied

coolly. "After all, she's been the matriarch of that family for almost two hundred years."

"She threatened me that if I didn't come clean, she'd tell the family at her party to make an example of me," he seethed. "Can you imagine what that would have done to Avonne, her own granddaughter?"

I had to agree that Hattie's plan wasn't ideal. Then again, Stone wasn't exactly winning any personality contests. Either way, the answer wasn't murder.

"You can't kill us both," I said. "Don't you know who we are?"

Stone laughed. "I killed Hattie Rollins-Mahoney. Do you really think I have a problem taking out a Rose or two? I don't care what your name is, doll. The only thing you are is an obstacle to be overcome by whatever means necessary."

I had flashbacks to my New Jersey apartment and the maniacal mobster that had come to kill Marley and me. My cousins had saved me then. Linnea, Aster, and Florian had dropped down into my living room like stars from the sky. I'd been in awe of them, not realizing that I possessed the same powers as my magical cousins. If only I could send off a beacon now, but I knew that was impossible thanks to Stone's quick thinking.

Raoul? Are you there? No reply and no sign of the trash panda. A wave of nausea crashed over me. I couldn't let anything happen to Marley. She was my heart and soul. She represented all that was good in the world—the opposite of this evil wereass in front of me. She deserved to have her whole life ahead of her.

The blade of a large knife glinted in the moonlight. "I can make it look like an attack. Maybe the shifter community will be blamed." He threw back his head and laughed. "Oh, your poor boyfriend. That sheriff should've been a little better at his job. How badly will it hurt him to realize he could have saved you by actually solving the murder?"

I couldn't think about Granger right now. All I could think about was Marley. "Please let my daughter go. She won't tell anyone, I swear. She's a very responsible girl. Always does as she's told."

"Except buying potions behind her mom's back," Stone said. "I know all about that place. Why do you think I went there for my potion? It's off the beaten track. He doesn't tend to serve the adult community, if you know what I mean."

Which is why the sheriff didn't even check there for the potion. Maybe he didn't even know about its existence. I'd never noticed it before.

"How did you steal the key from Sampson?" I asked.

"I didn't," Stone said. "That was my plan, but when I went to his room, I couldn't find it."

"Because he carried the keys on his person during the day," I said. "And that's when you searched his room."

He squinted. "How do you know when I checked the room?"

"Because Sampson only left the key in his drawer when he was in the bedroom at night." I paused. "So you must've snuck the potion into the glass of mead during the party."

"Sure did," he boasted. "No one notices when I'm not around because they assume I'm on a work call. I took the opportunity to slip into the dining room while everyone was on the portico."

"And you loosened the chandelier, but you never intended to kill her that way."

He laughed. "No, that was to throw everyone off my scent. I mean, I saved her. Why would I then immediately turn around and kill her? It was like an alibi."

"Except you made enough mistakes that your alibi doesn't matter," I said.

"And I'm rectifying those mistakes right now," he sneered. Thunder boomed overhead, followed by a flash of lightning. Stone glanced skyward. "What in Zeus's name? It's not supposed to storm tonight. I checked my weather app before I chose this place." He seemed genuinely annoyed that Mother Nature hadn't adhered to his guidelines. What a nut job.

I clucked my tongue. "All these unruly women," I said. "Does no one do your bidding?"

He kicked me hard in the leg and I winced. "Do you want your death to be slow or quick? I was intending to be merciful but that can change." A slow grin emerged. "Even better, I can start with your daughter. I'll be kind enough to let Mom watch."

I strained against the ropes. "Don't you touch a hair on that girl's head or I will come back from the grave and make your life a misery. Such is the power of the One True Witch."

Thunder rolled again and another lightning strike succeeded it.

"Can't say I'm very impressed with what I've seen so far," he said. He brandished his knife and crouched beside me. "Would you like me to bring her over here or would you prefer to move over there?"

I spat in his eye. "I'd like you to untie me, so I can kick your troll-sized ass."

He rose to his full height and swung his arm back, just as thunder pealed again. Lightning cracked the sky and made contact with his metal blade. Stone's entire body snapped and fizzled. He dropped the knife and clutched his chest before collapsing in a heap.

"Mom!" Marley bypassed Stone and dropped to her knees beside me. She set to work untying my bindings.

"Marley, thank the gods," I breathed. "How did you get

loose? Is Raoul here?" I scanned the area behind her for any sign of my furry friend.

"No, I did it myself." Her face was shining.

It was then that I became aware of the silence. No thunder. No lightning bolts. The storm had stopped as quickly as it had started. I glanced up to see that the sliver of moon was visible again, pinned to its dark blanket. I'd had that experience once before, when I'd broken through the suppression spell my father had placed on my magic. My spirits lifted.

"Marley Rose," I said, bursting with joy. "Did you use magic?"

She threw her arms around me. "I did! I feel it, Mom. It's the craziest sensation." She studied her arms as though she could see the magic coursing through her veins.

"How did you make the storm happen?" I asked.

"I didn't do it on purpose," she said. "I was panicking that he was going to kill you and that I had to save you, and my body practically exploded."

I kissed her forehead. "Well, I think Stone is the one who exploded." I peered over her shoulder at the still body on the ground. I had no idea whether he was unconscious or dead. Right now, I didn't care. My daughter was safe and that was all that mattered.

Marley gave me a sly grin. "What was that thing you said earlier about not wanting me to harm anyone for your sake?"

Cheeky girl. "There is an implied life-or-death exception to that statement."

The crunch of leaves told us that we weren't alone. I squinted between the trees to see the glow of amber eyes. A large wolf stepped into the clearing. He paused next to the body and observed the knife. I knew what was coming next.

"Avert your eyes, Marley," I said quickly.

The wolf shifted into the sheriff. It didn't hurt that he was stark naked and looked damn good standing there.

"Granger," I said. Tears pricked my eyes.

He rushed forward, his expression a mixture of relief and worry. "What in the hell happened, Rose?"

Marley turned toward him with her hand over her eyes. "Maybe someone can magic you a pair of pants and then we can talk."

"I don't have my wand," I said. "I left it in the car."

"Nobody panic," Deputy Bolan's voice cut through the darkness. "I've got his emergency clothes right here. He's not an easy wolf to follow when he's moving that fast." The leprechaun tossed a drawstring bag at the sheriff.

"I wasn't panicked," I said. "In fact, I was enjoying the free show."

The sheriff leaned forward and kissed me before pulling the clothes from the bag and quickly putting them on. I burst into laughter at the sight of the T-shirt with a witch silhouette and the words 'Witch Slapped' emblazoned across the front. Even better, the shirt was paired with neon yellow shorts.

"Deputy, we need to have a word later about this emergency kit," the sheriff said.

The leprechaun stifled a laugh. "I didn't pack this one, boss."

"Can you find out if Stone is dead?" I asked.

"He's alive, but barely," the sheriff replied.

"The healer is on the way," Deputy Bolan said. "As soon as the sheriff got a hit on your location, we called the healer's office. We didn't know what state we'd find you in."

"How did you find us?" I asked. I wasn't even sure which part of Starry Hollow we were in.

"I found your car unlocked," the sheriff said. "No way would Rose leave her car unlocked, I said. She's too suspicious of everyone to do a trusting thing like that."

I smiled. "So you decided to go full wolf?"

"It was the fastest way to track your scent," he replied.

"Stone killed Hattie," Marley said. "Mom figured it out, so he planned to kill us, too."

I heard a low growl as the sheriff's gaze flickered to the body and back to us. "I'm sorry I didn't get here sooner, Rose."

"You couldn't have known," I said. "He covered his tracks really well."

"Not well enough for you," the sheriff said. "How'd you manage to knock him out?"

I smiled broadly at my daughter. "Ask this one here."

"I came into my magic," Marley announced proudly.

"You're kidding." The sheriff pulled Marley in for a hug. "Look at you, little witch. Taking after your mama already."

"It must've been a psychological barrier after all," Marley said.

Deputy Bolan nudged Stone's arm with his tip of his boot. "He's really out. What'd you do to him?"

"Electrocuted him with lightning," Marley said, completely blasé.

Deputy Bolan whistled. "Stars and stones."

"Starry Hollow had better watch out," I said. "I think she's going to be one powerful witch. Aunt Hyacinth is going to lose her kaftan."

Marley clapped her hands. "Black Cloak Academy, here I come! This is the best belated birthday present ever." She glanced down at the locket around her neck. "Sorry, Dad. You're cool, too, but my heart was set on being a witch like Mom."

The sound of the healer's voice echoed through the forest.

"We're here, Cephas," the sheriff called.

The healer appeared in the clearing and immediately took in the scene. "I think I can guess who won the fight. I take it he's alive?"

The sheriff's expression darkened. "He's lucky I'm a law-abiding citizen."

"That's kind of implied with that shiny star you usually wear," I said.

He gave me a gruff kiss on top of the head before joining Cephas by the body. The three men got busy with the suspect and the crime scene, while Marley and I continued to sit huddled together against the large live oak, waiting for a ride home. The live oaks were beautiful trees that my father had mentioned often enough during my childhood that I knew about them. He'd lived here most of his life, with his beloved trees and his magic. Then briefly with his wife and his daughter. And now I was here with mine. It struck me that the circle of life wasn't perfectly round. It was more of a weird zigzag pattern that eventually reunited with its beginning.

"Thank you for saving me," I said.

"You'd have done the same for me," Marley replied.

"Never doubt that for a second." I heaved a sigh of gratitude for this moment. To have my daughter not only alive and well, but thriving. "I'm so proud of you, not just for the way you handled Stone, but for the way you are all the time. You're a remarkable young woman, Marley, and the world is fortunate to have you."

Marley elbowed me gently. "You're only saying that because I'm your daughter."

"No, you're much more than that, Marley Rose," I said, placing a kiss on her forehead. "You're my hero."

CHAPTER EIGHTEEN

"I CAN'T WAIT to stay the night at Linnea's," Marley said. "Bryn and Hudson are going to go nuts when they see me with my wand." She brandished the antique wand given to her by Aunt Hyacinth.

"Be careful with that wand, Marley," I said. "That's a family heirloom."

"I know," Marley said, whooshing it around the room. "I can't believe she gave it to me. Why not her own kids?"

"That's something you'll have to ask Aunt Hyacinth."

"Can you teach me how to change the color of the flowers outside?" Marley asked. "I want to do rainbow colors."

I glanced hesitantly at the clock. Granger was due in less than an hour and I still needed to get ready. I knew Linnea and Rick would be here soon to pick up Marley. At least her bag was packed.

"We can do a few minutes, but that's it," I said.

Marley lifted PP3 off the sofa. "You can watch," she said.

"Bring his leash," I said. "You never know when he'll get a second wind."

"Mom, he's ten," Marley said. "Even if he gets a second

wind, that only means he'll move at slightly faster than a glacial pace. Besides, we both have magic now. We can trap him in a bubble or something." She rubbed her nose against his. "Right, boy? Magic bubbles!"

We left the cottage and wandered over to the nearest flower patch by the white picket fence. I produced my wand. "Which color first?" I asked.

"Purple stripes," Marley said. "I want patterns, too."

"Oh, boy. Creative and magical." I shook my head. "I'm frightened already."

At the word 'frightened,' Marley's expression clouded over. "So Mom, is Stone going to recover from the lightning strike?"

I realized that she felt conflicted about what she'd done to him. "Yes, sweetheart. He's alive and well, and going to spend the rest of his life in prison."

"There's enough evidence to convict him?" she asked hopefully.

"The sheriff thinks so," I said. "There's his confession to us and the proof of purchase of the potion from Devil's Claw. The ingredients exactly match what was found in Hattie's system. Turns out there's no such company as Pippin Enterprises in Starlight City either. The whole story about a company buying him out was a fabrication. And Fern is willing to testify about her relationship with him."

"He seemed so nice in the shop," Marley said. "He let me go first."

"Probably to minimize eyes on his purchase," I said. "The sheriff spoke to the gardener, too, and he can testify that he saw Stone in Sampson's room the day of the murder, probably searching for the key to the cellar. He didn't realize it was Stone at the time. He only saw the brightly colored shirt."

"But I thought he didn't end up using the key," Marley said.

"He didn't," I said. "But every bit of evidence helps the case against him."

"I feel sad for his family," Marley said. "The kids are going to be without their dad."

I tipped up her chin. "Marley Rose, you are not responsible for that tree nymph's imprisonment. He *chose* to murder someone. Premeditated. The worst kind."

"Between this and Holly, you were right," Marley said. "Magic doesn't make everything easier."

"But sometimes it does." I glanced at the flowers. "Which color and pattern did you say? Purple stripes?" As I raised my wand, PP3 began to bark and run in a circle.

"What is it, boy?" Marley asked, kneeling beside him.

I tried to figure out what had the Yorkie so spooked, but he was too excited and kept bumping into Marley's leg as he ran.

A little mother-daughter magic before the real magic happens? Raoul appeared from the side of the cottage.

I don't know what you're talking about, I said.

I saw the kid's overnight bag and the new candle you bought, the raccoon said. *I know what that means.*

Stop snooping!

"Oh, PP3, that's just Raoul," Marley said, petting the dog. "You know him."

PP3 had no interest in the raccoon. He continued to bark.

Uh oh. Incoming, Raoul said, looking skyward.

"Incoming?" I repeated, confused. I followed Raoul's gaze to a small gray and white object in the sky. The winged object was careening toward us at a high rate of speed.

"Duck!" Marley yelled.

We all ducked as the creature swooped over us. It circled back and landed on the fence post. I dared to lift my head and saw the cutest winged kitten in the history of adorable kittens.

"Bonkers!" Marley exclaimed. Her excitement was contagious. She ran to the creature and kissed the top of its head.

"A random flying cat really is bonkers," I said.

"No, that's her name," Marley corrected me. "Bonkers. I know because she told me." She beamed proudly, stroking the kitten's delicate wings. PP3 looked about ready to have a stroke.

I looked from Marley to the winged kitten. "She's…?"

Marley nodded. "That's right. Bonkers is my familiar."

I didn't have time to process this development because Linnea pulled into the driveway, ready to take Marley back to Palmetto House for the night.

"Can Bonkers come, please?" Marley begged.

If Linnea was surprised to see a winged kitten on the fence post, she didn't show it. "Of course," Linnea said. "What kind of witch would I be to separate you from your familiar?"

"You can do me that favor whenever you like," I said wryly.

Raoul glowered at me.

"Where's Rick?" Marley asked.

"Back at the house with the kids," Linnea said. "They're in the middle of building a house of cards and I risked the entire operation if Rick left."

"I'll be right back," Marley said. "I need to get my bag." She dashed into the cottage, leaving the door open behind her.

"Thanks so much for having her," I said.

"Our pleasure," Linnea said. "I'm so happy her magic finally manifested. What do you think was the holdup? The potion she used on Holly?" I'd already told Florian about Marley's actions, which he'd clearly passed along to his sister.

"Based on what the therapist said, a psychological block is the most likely culprit," I replied. "Marley had a lot of conflicting emotions. She felt guilty about what she'd done to Holly and, on top of that, she'd been building up her birthday in her mind for so long that the reality became too much for her. She became frightened of her own potential."

"So how'd she manage to break through the block?" Linnea asked.

"The same way I broke through the suppression spell back in New Jersey," I said. "Unconditional love."

Linnea smiled. "She'll make an exceptional member of the coven, like her mother."

My laugh turned into a cough. "I don't think you've been reading Hazel's reports."

"Hazel is a middle-aged curmudgeon," Linnea replied. "I'm sure you're making great strides. If you don't mind, I can show her a few spells while she's over. I think it will be nice for me to have someone to share magic with."

I felt an unexpected pang of guilt. It never occurred to me that Linnea might feel wistful over her children not inheriting magic. I only knew how it affected her relationship with Aunt Hyacinth.

"Marley would absolutely love that," I said. "I can tell I'm going to have a hard time keeping up with her."

Marley emerged with her bag in tow. "Ready! Come on, Bonkers."

The winged kitten flew to the car but settled on the roof.

"I think she intends to follow by air," I said.

PP3 ran to the car and growled. A raccoon, a Yorkie, and a winged kitten. Rose Cottage was going to have quite the menagerie.

"Winged cats are very rare," Linnea said. "This is a good omen. Mother will be pleased."

"Marley's pleased," I said. "And that's really all I care about."

Linnea smiled. "You're so right, Ember." She squeezed my arm. "Have fun tonight. Say hi to Granger for me."

Did everyone in Starry Hollow know what tonight entailed? Argh! "I will." I kissed Marley before she got into the car. "Remember your manners."

"I'm not the one who needs reminding," Marley said sweetly. She climbed into the passenger seat and blew me another kiss. I waved until the car and its flying kitten companion were out of sight. My daughter had a familiar of her own. I could hardly believe it.

Boom-chicka-bow-wow. Raoul began to gyrate in a circle.

Stop! I ordered. *You're banished for the night. Go submerge yourself in garbage. Cover your face in banana peels and call it a facial.*

No need to be rude, he sulked. *Fine. I'm going, but I'll be back bright and early for the details.*

"No details!" One menacing look from me and he took off for the woods. I hurried into the house to prepare for my date with the hottest werewolf in town.

I darted upstairs and changed out of my clothes, slipping on a sheer white robe and nothing else. I spritzed perfume and then used a quick spell to turn on Bruce Springsteen and set the mood. I danced around the room with my wand, shooting magical energy wherever I saw fit. I used a spell to fix my hair and makeup. I even used magic to light a candle—the height of decadence—or maybe laziness. The jury was out on that one.

When the doorbell finally rang, I used a spell to open the front door so that I could maintain the boudoir mood. I was surprised I didn't hear a peep from PP3 downstairs. He usually growled at the sheriff. I smiled to myself. Even the dog was finally getting on board.

"I'm upstairs," I yelled. I positioned myself on the bed and tried to find my sexiest pose. What a time to discover that I didn't really have a sexy pose. I lowered my head so that my hair dipped over my eye. Thin strands of hair immediately got tangled in my eyelashes and I tried to pull them out before the sheriff saw me. When I glanced up, it wasn't the sheriff looming in the doorway.

It was Alec.

The beating of my heart screeched to a halt. His usual crisp, custom suit was askew, his shirt unbuttoned, and his tie hung loose around his neck. His fangs extended at the sight of me sprawled across the bed in nothing except a sheer white robe.

I grabbed the nearest pillow in an attempt to cover myself. "Alec, what are you doing here?" My pulse was racing as he moved to stand at the edge of the bed.

"I cannot begin to tell you how much I've missed you," he said quietly. His eyes never left me. "I made a terrible mistake with Holly. I never should have allowed myself to enter that relationship. It was meant as a diversion. The truth is that my feelings for you..." He cleared his throat. I'd never seen him in such a state before. "I've come to apologize and humbly ask...to ask for more. I'm ready, Miss Rose...Ember."

A lump formed in my throat. *Now?* I was finally ready to give myself over to Granger and *now* Alec wanted a chance with me? I gaped at him in disbelief.

"Alec, I don't know what to say," I said. "I wasn't expecting you or...this."

"Please." His expression was a mixture of pain, grief, and longing. I knew it well because I'd worn it myself on many occasions.

"Granger is on his way," I said absently. My mind went blank. All I could do was stare at the gorgeous vampire at the edge of my bed, begging me for a chance. For a future. Sweet baby Elvis. Why was life so complicated? My head swam with confusion.

PP3's growl downstairs brought me to my senses. I sat up, fully alert. "You have to go," I said. "Granger can't see you in here. He won't understand." I wasn't sure I understood.

"I'm here, Rose," the sheriff called from downstairs. "Where are you? Playing hide-and-seek? Because I'm up for it."

My eyes were glued to Alec. I suddenly recalled my aunt's words from Marley's party—walls were quick to go up but slow to come down. It wasn't only true of her. I reached for my wand on the nightstand and did a spell to change my clothes from sexy to casual. Relief rippled across the vampire's features.

"Hurry up before your wiry beast slays me," the sheriff yelled.

I aimed my wand at the window and opened it. "You can leave that way."

Alec nodded wordlessly and jumped from the window with the grace of an angel. My heart burned.

"Give me a minute," I yelled. "I'll be right down."

I turned off the music and doused the flame.

* * *

ALSO BY ANNABEL CHASE

Sign up for my newsletter and receive a FREE short story that introduces Raoul and Ember: http://eepurl.com/ctYNzf

Other Books By Annabel Chase—

Spellbound

Curse the Day, Book 1

Doom and Broom, Book 2

Spell's Bells, Book 3

Lucky Charm, Book 4

Better Than Hex, Book 5

Cast Away, Book 6

A Touch of Magic, Book 7

A Drop in the Potion, Book 8

Hemlocked and Loaded, Book 9

All Spell Breaks Loose, Book 10

Spellbound Ever After

Crazy For Brew, Book 1

Lost That Coven Feeling, Book 2

Wands Upon A Time, Book 3

Spellslingers Academy of Magic

Outcast, Warden of the West, Book 1

Outclassed, Warden of the West, Book 2

Outlast, Warden of the West, Book 3

Printed in Great Britain
by Amazon